'A tender tale about ageing, o▓ ▓▓▓▓
brutality of love. About wha▓ ▓▓▓▓
human is, about fathers a▓ ▓▓▓▓
The kind of book you give t▓ ▓▓▓▓
to say "I've been thinking ▓▓▓▓
**Fredrik Backman, ▓**

'There are not many novels that I want to tell you that you
should read, but this is one of them. It is a novel about
family, how our history shapes our present, and the many
different forms that love can take. This is a beautiful and
gentle novel . . . and I won't ever forget it.'
**NB Magazine**

'*When the Cranes Fly South* really touched me . . . and
Sixten completely stole my heart. This story felt universal
and timeless – it's about love and death and family and
friendship. Everything that makes us human.'
**Josie Ferguson, author of *The Silence in Between***

'The most moving book I've ever read – heart-breaking
but also heartwarming'
**Jacqueline Wilson**

'Lisa Ridzén's debut demonstrates how sometimes the
simplest storytelling can be the most effective. Anyone
anywhere who has worried for a crumbling parent, or worried
about the crumble in themselves, or simply worried that their
dog understood them better than their family,
will identify with Ridzén's novel.'
**Patrick Gale, *Guardian***

'Once you've read this beautiful and deeply emotional story,
you'll want to pass it on to someone you love.'
**Fabulous Magazine**

'Lucid, observant . . . a heartfelt novel that gives
voice to a sensitively realized old man.'
***Irish Times***

'This profoundly moving novel is sure to melt you into tears
faster than a Cornetto in the sunshine.'
***Woman & Home***

'Meditations on memory and fatherhood underpin this tender
tale about a man defending his right to live independently.'
***Financial Times***

'Prepare to be emotionally hijacked.'
***Grazia***

'A magical reading experience; among the most moving
things I've ever read . . . I know this novel will always
have a place in my heart.'
**Camilla Läckberg, author of *The Hidden Child***

'Irresistible. So tender and moving. It's as if Fredrik Backman's
*Ove* had a love child with Åsa Larsson's *Sivving*.'
**Malin Persson Giolito, author of *Beyond
All Reasonable Doubt***

'A powerful read about righting wrongs before it's too late.'
***Good Housekeeping***

'A powerful, sneakily emotional meditation on life
and death, and the foundational relationships in our lives.
This is a book that will echo in your soul.'
**Garth Stein, author of *The Art of Racing in the Rain***

# When the Cranes Fly South

*Lisa Ridzén*

Translated from Swedish by Alice Menzies

PENGUIN BOOKS

TRANSWORLD PUBLISHERS

UK | USA | Canada | Ireland | Australia
India | New Zealand | South Africa

Transworld is part of the Penguin Random House group of companies
whose addresses can be found at global.penguinrandomhouse.com.

Penguin Random House UK, One Embassy Gardens, 8 Viaduct Gardens, London SW11 7BW

penguin.co.uk

First published in Great Britain in 2025 by Doubleday
an imprint of Transworld Publishers
Penguin paperback edition published 2026

006

Copyright © Lisa Ridzén 2024
English translation copyright © Alice Menzies 2024

The cost of this translation was supported by a subsidy from
the Swedish Arts Council, gratefully acknowledged.

The moral right of the author has been asserted

Typeset in Arno Pro by Six Red Marbles UK, Thetford, Norfolk.
Printed and bound in Great Britain by Clays Ltd, Elcograf S.p.A.

The authorized representative in the EEA is Penguin Random House Ireland,
Morrison Chambers, 32 Nassau Street, Dublin D02 YH68.

A CIP catalogue record for this book is available from the British Library

ISBN: 9781804995808

Penguin Random House is committed to a sustainable future
for our business, our readers and our planet. This book is made
from Forest Stewardship Council® certified paper.

For Cameron

How lucky we are to have each other

# Thursday
# 18 May

I FANTASIZE about cutting him out of my will, making sure he doesn't get a penny.

He claims it's as much for my sake as Sixten's that he wants to take him away. That old men like me shouldn't be trudging about in the woods, and that dogs like Sixten need longer walks than a quick stroll to the road and back.

I look down at Sixten, who is curled up beside me on the daybed. He lets out a big yawn and gets himself comfortable with his head on my belly. I dig my swollen fingers into his coat and shake my head. What does that idiot know, anyway? There's no chance in hell I'm going to let him get his own way.

At the kitchen table, Ingrid sighs.

'I can't promise anything, Bo, but I'll do my best. This isn't OK,' she says, scribbling away in the carers' log book.

I nod and give her a faint smile. If there's anyone who can help me with Sixten, it's Ingrid.

The fire crackles, and I struggle to tear my eyes away from the flames dancing around the birch logs. My thoughts drift back to the conversation I had with Hans this morning, and I feel myself getting worked up again. Who does he think he is, our son? It's not up to him to decide where Sixten should live.

I close my eyes for a moment, tired from all the anger. I listen to Ingrid's movements, and my breathing gradually slows as the rage subsides.

In its wake, I'm left with the same niggling feeling I've experienced quite often lately. A clawing that comes and goes in my chest. A sense that I should be doing things differently.

'God, you've become a real brooder,' Ture said on the phone recently, when I tried to explain.

He's probably right, I think now, lying here beside Sixten and listening to Ingrid pottering about.

Because in the void you left behind, Fredrika, I've started thinking about things I never paid much attention to. I've never been one to doubt myself, always known what I want and been able to tell right from wrong. I still can, but I've also started to wonder.

I've started to wonder why things worked out the way they did. To think about my mother and my old man in a way I never have before. But more than anything, I've been thinking about Hans. I don't want things between us to end up the way they did with my old man.

It's just that all his nagging about Sixten makes me so angry I don't know what to do with myself. I won't be able to fix a single bloody thing if he takes Sixten away.

'I'll go for a quick walk with him at lunch,' Ingrid says, as she firmly closes the log book.

Her little eyes flash. She has a dog of her own, and just the thought of Sixten being taken away upsets her. She runs a hand through her short grey hair and picks up my pill organizer. Checks that everything is right. For my heart and all the rest of it.

'Thank you,' I say, taking a sip of my tea.

If we'd had a daughter, I would have liked her to be like Ingrid. She was in the same year at school as Hans, and her grandfather worked at the sawmill in Ranviken at the same time as my old man.

She wasn't wearing a jacket when she arrived today, just the navy fleece with the home help company's logo on the chest, and

I can't believe she's not cold. That sort of thing always surprises me nowadays, that no one ever seems to feel the cold. I used to go without socks for half the year, and I'd be in shorts from the start of May, but these days I'm freezing all the time. The doctors and carers tell me that's just what happens. That it's normal. It doesn't matter that the weather is getting warmer, I'm going to keep lighting the fire.

You've always been a nesh soul, Fredrika, shivering at the slightest chill. They usually have you wearing one of your old woollen cardigans whenever we come to visit.

Ingrid frowns, and I think I hear her mutter something about the pre-packaged pills. One day, she'll start shivering like an emaciated goat too.

She double checks the organizer one last time, then takes out her phone to see if anyone has called. It strikes me that I don't know whether she has a family of her own – or have I just forgotten? I've noticed from the way people reply to my questions that I'm getting forgetful. It really seems to bother Hans.

'You just asked me that,' he always snaps.

Ingrid never makes me feel foolish like that.

I study her as I shift my legs, stretched out on one of your old patchwork quilts. I'm sure she has beautiful children. Friendly and well raised.

I reach for the glass of rosehip soup she left on the table earlier and drink a big mouthful of the cool, thick liquid. Rosehip is one of the few flavours I still enjoy. So many other things taste different nowadays. I can't eat cream cakes any more, for example, because they taste like mould, but Hans still insists on buying them.

'You're getting so thin,' he says. As though it's my fault my muscles are wasting away. As though I invented the ageing, useless body.

I set the glass back down on the table and use my lower lip to suck the soup from my moustache.

Ingrid goes over to the stove and adds a couple of logs. She knows what she's doing. She and that brother of hers have a firewood processor, the kind that can cut and split the wood. Twelve tonnes it weighs. I didn't know her parents, but I know who they were. Both died early, and Ingrid took over the family farm.

Some of the other carers have no idea how to light a fire, and they always put the birch bark at the bottom rather than building a stack and lighting it from the top. I used to correct them, but after a while I got sick of doing that. The young ones in particular feel like a lost cause. There's plenty I could say about my old man, but at least he taught me how to light a fire properly. Young people today, they don't think any further than tomorrow. They get everything served up to them on a platter, and they can't do any of the things we learned as kids. What would they do if something big happened? If the power went out, or the water supply failed? They'd collapse like a house of cards, the lot of them.

My gaze comes to rest on the fire again. I think I'd probably be able to last a good while on water from the stream, burning logs in the stove and eating the food stored in the basement. The flames nibble tentatively at the birch bark and quickly grow into a raging blaze. The flickering glow makes me think of Hans and the way he used to sit transfixed in front of the fire as a boy. Back when he still looked up to me and pricked his ears at everything I said.

'Hans says I should stop using the stove, too. He doesn't just want to take Sixten away; he wants to take my wood as well.' I chuckle, though the familiar clawing feeling in my chest is back. 'He thinks I should just turn the radiators up, that I can afford it.'

'I know,' Ingrid replies, rinsing off a plate. 'But it's from a place of concern, you know that. He's worried you might forget about the damper or fall while you're bringing in the wood, when you've been out with Sixten.'

Or maybe it's just selfishness and pig-headed idiocy, I think, though I bite my tongue.

'Don't worry about the wood, Bo. We're here so often that if you need anything, we'll realize soon enough.'

I reach up and touch my beard, mutter that Hans doesn't give two hoots about them being here, but Ingrid doesn't seem to hear.

'It'll be Eva-Lena this evening,' she says after a while.

I feel a rush of anger and nod with my eyes closed, but I know sleep will have me in its relaxing grip before long.

Eva-Lena started coming over when Ingrid slipped on the first ice and broke her foot. She was off work for weeks, which meant I had to put up with that stroppy battle-axe instead – and as if that weren't enough, she's from Frösön.

They visit me four times a day, the home help. When Hans first broached the idea, about six months after you left, I thought it was ridiculous. I laughed in his face, in fact, though I did feel bad afterwards. He meant well, I suppose.

This was back when I was still in control of my own life.

I'm lucky I have Ture. He's been dealing with the carers for much longer than me. One of the doctors forced them on to him when he went to hospital after a fall. Some young whippersnapper who said he was worried that Ture lived alone and didn't have anyone to help with his shopping. It didn't matter that he'd spent most of his life living alone; Ture soon found himself with people running about the house every few hours.

The shower is one part of it he doesn't like. I don't really care about them seeing me naked, but Ture finds it uncomfortable. Says he feels sorry for anyone who has to look at his rickety old body.

No, what bothers me most is my lack of balance. If it was a bit better, taking Sixten for longer walks would be a piece of cake. There wouldn't be any fuss over him, and I wouldn't have to get so angry with Hans.

Aside from Ingrid, Johanna is my favourite. She's around Ellinor's age, from over Bölviken way. Big and loud, just like that mother of hers. You never know what might come out of her mouth, and she makes me laugh even though I don't have much to laugh about now. Ture seems to have different temps every other day, but if that were me I'd be straight on the damn phone to the head of the council. Is it too much to ask not to have complete strangers marching in and out of your house?

'I'll add a couple of logs before I go, so you can doze off if you want,' Ingrid tells me as she gets up from the kitchen table. I hadn't even noticed her sit down.

She clears away the plate and cutlery she used to cut my sandwich into bite-sized pieces. I have only two teeth left at the bottom, and it takes me a long time to eat unless she cuts things up. Hans has been nagging me to get a dental bridge fitted, but I don't see the point. A waste of money for such a short period of time. Besides, the soft cheese they give me isn't too bad. Not quite as good as the firmer stuff, but we can't have everything.

Sixten presses up against my leg, and I feel an ache in my chest. A sudden urge to talk to you. Not that we were ever people who talked a lot. You would say that of course I'm still capable of bringing in the wood and taking the dog for a walk, that it's enough to go over to the edge of the trees and let him do his business.

It's been over three years since you moved away, since you gave me that look of such complete confusion when our son came to get you. He said it was time to go and that you'd be better off there.

I could tell you didn't believe him. That you would rather stay here with me, where everything was familiar. I let you rest in my gaze for a moment, and I wanted nothing more than for you to stay. But then I took your hand, gave it a gentle squeeze, and said:

'Hans is right, you'll be much happier there.'

Every single fibre of me disagreed, but I knew I couldn't take care of you.

I cast a quick glance at the jar on the table and then at Ingrid. Can't open it myself; my fingers are too stiff and weak to grip the lid. My hands are still as big as hams, but the strength is gone and I can't bend my fingers properly.

'Sausage fingers are normal for someone your age and with your medical history,' the doctor told me the last time I was there.

Ingrid tried to find a jar that would be easier to open but still secure enough to stop your scent from disappearing, but I couldn't manage that either.

'Do you need help with the jar?' she asks with her back to me.

I quickly lower my eyes. She has helped me with it so many times, but it's still embarrassing. Keeping your dementia-addled wife's scarf in a jar just to be able to remember her scent is fundamentally pathetic, after all. That's why Ingrid is the only one who knows about it. I'd be embarrassed even in front of you. We weren't the kind of people to whisper sweet nothings in each other's ear. We never needed that sort of thing.

Ingrid opens the lid and hands the jar to me, then turns around and continues to wipe the worktop.

I inhale deeply through the fabric. Close my eyes and let my eyelids trap the burning sensation. No one has ever told me that it's normal for a person's eyes to well up so easily as they age, for the tears to find a foothold in virtually every memory.

You bought the scarf at a spring market in town, back when Hans was still too young to walk on his own. He was in the pushchair we'd inherited from the neighbours on the other side of the road. I remember its big wheels. Perfect for walking on gravel, you said. The scarf was dark red to begin with, but over the years you mended it with lots of little multicoloured patches. Whenever it was cold, you would wrap it around your neck, and if it was warm you would tie it around your shoulders.

'Don't you want to take this?' I asked as you were leaving the house for the last time, after Hans had helped you pack a bag for Brunkullagården.

You turned around, and for a split second I thought you were back with me, that you would say thank you and smile the way you always did when I remembered something you'd forgotten. But you just stared at me with a blank expression on your face, as though I were holding a foreign object in my hand.

I don't dare keep the scarf out of the jar for too long, because I want the scent to last. You smell so different now that they've swapped your soaps and creams. Your brain isn't the only thing the dementia has changed.

I shove the scarf into the jar and manage to screw the lid back into place. I then set it down on the table so that Ingrid can tighten it, and lean my head against the pillow.

The sound of her doing the dishes is like a lullaby, and I get lost in the fire, barely notice when she says goodbye and closes the door behind her.

The summer nights are starting to get brighter, but the kitchen is dark. There are only a couple of small windows in here, and the brown ceiling swallows any light that does manage to get in.

The fire is still crackling, Sixten breathing heavily. I scratch him behind the ear and on his neck. His fur there is as soft and downy as it was all over when he was a pup. You were sceptical when the Fredrikssons asked if we wanted a new puppy. He would be the seventh dog we had got from them. They must have bred at least a hundred elkhounds for helping with the hunt. You thought we were too old for another one, and Hans agreed. I thought the pair of you were ridiculous and called you both pessimists.

At dinner one day, I snapped and asked what the hell the point of life was if I was too old for a dog. Were we just supposed to sit around, waiting to die? A few days later, Hans gave us a ride over to the Fredrikssons' place in Fåker, and when I lifted Sixten and put him into your arms, you changed your mind too. You even went down to the Larssons' and got a bit of liver to dry, so we'd have something to train him with. That was almost exactly a year before we noticed the first symptoms.

I loosely grip Sixten's ear, and he snores softly. The movement makes me think about just how stiff my fingers are. I had to stop taking my rheumatism medication when I first started taking the pills for my heart.

'When it really comes down to it, it's not a hard choice between your heart and your joints, is it?' the locum doctor had asked with a smile.

Dying of a heart attack probably wouldn't be a bad way to go, I had time to think, before he interrupted my thoughts.

'Unless you have any other questions, I think we're done for today,' he said, turning to his screen.

The intensity of his fingers on the keyboard made it sound as if he was in a hurry, as if he had somewhere better to be. His thin grey hair was like an ugly shower cap on his round head. Had to be approaching retirement, I thought. I'd heard that locum doctors earn as much in one month as I did in a year at the sawmill. When I asked where my usual doctor was, this new one started telling me about himself, that his mother came from Jämtland. As though I cared.

I wanted to get up, to bring my cane down on the desk and ask how the hell it could be considered normal to have hands that can't even open the lid of a herring jar. To have to choose between that and dropping down dead. But the words I was looking for floated away, out of reach.

I wished that Hans would get up and say that we refused to accept this. That he could take me by the arm and fix everything – the way I did when the neighbour's lad was throwing pinecones at him by the bus stop. Grabbed the boy's sweater and shoved him in the ditch. But Hans just passed me my jacket and got to his feet, and then we drove home.

Sixten snores loudly, and I squeeze his ear. I can still manage a pretty good grip between my thumb and fingers. Ingrid tells me I have a harder nip than most eighty-nine-year-olds, but your hands are tougher, Fredrika. The staff at Brunkullagården told me that. I should probably be ashamed, but it makes me happy to hear that you pinch them so hard your knuckles turn white.

*1.30 p.m.*

*Bo wanted fish gratin for lunch, plus coffee with lots of sugar. Blew into the bottle to loosen the phlegm and talked about Sixten. Wants me to write that he's upset because certain people think he should be rehomed. Fire OK.*

*Ingrid*

# Saturday
# 20 May

*12.30 p.m.*

*Grub o'clock: hash and beetroot. Bo's eyes bothering him, says they're going dark. Need to contact district nurse on Monday.*

*Kalle*

I WAKE to a warm sensation spreading across my crotch. Dreamed I was using the toilet, like Hans used to when he was little. Not much came out, but it's enough to make me uncomfortable.

I cast a quick glance at the clock on the wall. The carer will be here to make lunch soon, but I probably have time to go to the bathroom to change my underpants and trousers. They tell me I should wear nappies around the clock, but I always take them off the minute they leave. They think it's because I forget, but the truth is I'd rather pee myself and get changed than wear something like that.

I take a deep breath and force myself up from the daybed in the kitchen. There is a cold cup of tea on the table in front of me. One of the cups we bought on a trip out east, to the High Coast. You thought they were so nice, and though you said it wasn't necessary, I bought them for you because we'd just had a pay rise and I was feeling flush.

That was the summer Hans threw a party while we were away. He was stupid enough to make so much noise that they heard it all the way over at Marita and Nejla's place, and they told us, of course. My god, I gave him an earful once we got back, but he barely apologized. He'd started high school by that point and was hanging out with those boys from town. They put all sorts of ideas into his head – especially the lad from Frösön. Hans started talking back and asking questions about politics, telling us what he thought about what we did and the decisions we'd made. Questioning the most normal, obvious things.

'This is just what happens at that age,' you said one day, after he stormed off to his room and slammed the door.

'And that means he has to be insufferable too, does it?' I said, wiping my mouth with the sheet of kitchen roll you'd left beside my plate.

Earlier that spring, we'd locked horns over a language exchange trip, as he called it. He wanted to go to England to learn English over the summer, and he thought I should foot the bill. The boy from Frösön was going, which meant Hans wanted to go too, but I told him the truth: we couldn't afford something like that.

'Robert's dad can,' he snorted, acting like the biggest spoiled brat I'd ever seen.

I was so angry that everything went black. There was no way in hell I'd raised a snot-nosed kid who thought I should be paying for a jaunt to England, and I told him as much. That I didn't want to waste my money on such snobbishness.

You cleared the table. Stacked the dishes in silence and carried them over to the sink.

'You could try shouting and screaming a bit less yourself, you know,' you said after a moment or two, as you brought me a piece of sponge cake from the day before. 'And maybe that way he'd be less insufferable.'

I glared at you. Thought you should be taking my side.

Looking back now, I can see that you might have been right, but he just got me so bloody worked up. He knew exactly what to say to make me lose my head.

With a groan, I unbutton my jeans and let them drop to the bathroom floor, then study the wiry old man in the mirror. My eyes are stinging and I have trouble making out the details of my body. The figure in front of me looks more like an oil painting than anything, all crude brushstrokes, but my beard and long hair do stand out.

The sight makes me think of my old man. My face resembles his, though he was clean-shaven until the very end and never missed an opportunity to comment on my own lack of grooming.

'What a scruff you are,' he grunted one summer's evening, right as we were about to sit down to eat. I had just started my holiday, and you and I had come back from Hissmofors for a few days to help out on the farm. Mother had cooked herring and new potatoes with fresh dill from the garden.

During lunch break a couple of weeks earlier, Åkesson had announced he was going to grow a summer beard. 'A crate of beer to whoever comes back with the biggest one,' he said, putting his arms around me and P-G and thumping us both on the back.

'I'm in,' P-G had said with a grin. 'You've seen my dad, haven't you?'

I spat and said yes, that I'd seen his father's Santa beard.

'I'm in too,' I continued, thinking that you would probably complain about how scratchy it was.

That evening at the farm I had pulled out one of the garden chairs and sat down, studying my father without a word. You caught my eye from across the table and you held me there for a moment, allowing his grip over me to ease.

Mother served him a few spuds while you explained the bet I'd made with my workmates. He snorted something inaudible in reply and took a swig of beer while you turned to Mother and praised her food.

What he'd said about my beard was nothing but a throwaway remark, yet his words stayed with me. They always have. We sat quietly, my old man and me, looking down at our plates and eating Mother's food. Listening to you ask her about the crops and the animals. I was fascinated by how easily you could make conversation; you didn't seem to need to stop and think about what to say at all. I sipped my beer and glanced in my old man's direction.

My gaze kept slipping off his huge frame and no matter how hard I tried, I just couldn't bring myself to look him directly in the eye. I hated myself for that, for not being brave enough to speak up.

The stench of urine makes my nose sting as I drop my underpants to the floor. The carers have started leaving dry pants and trousers on the clothing rack in the corner, and I'm so grateful not to have to go into the bedroom to find fresh underwear. I haven't slept in there since you moved.

I reach for a pair of blue boxers and sit down on the toilet lid. Slowly bend forward and pull them over my left foot. The skin is mottled purple and blue, and my toes are crooked. My right foot is even stiffer than the left, but I manage to push it through the hole on the third attempt. I then grab a pair of trousers and start the whole process again. Tracksuit bottoms are easier than jeans, because they have more give. Hans must have bought me at least ten pairs from the Intersport in town.

I've just washed my hands and am about to turn off the tap when I hear the door open at the other end of the house. I find Kalle in the kitchen. He has already taken one of the ready meals out of the freezer, and he turns around as I come in. His clothes are too small for him, and his stomach peeps out whenever he moves. Behind him, I can see the note Hans put up above the worktop. REMEMBER TO EAT! I'll eat if I'm damn well hungry.

'How're we getting on today, then?' Kalle asks, stabbing holes in the plastic film over the ready meal. There's more food than I'd be able to eat in a year in the freezer, but Hans keeps buying more every week.

'Doing just fine, thanks,' I reply, wondering if he asks the same question to all the old folks he sees. It sounds a bit like a mantra.

'Thought I'd fix you up a bit of lunch. You hungry?'

I shrug and sit down beside Sixten on the daybed. Stroke his head.

Right then, the idea that something special is due to happen today pops into my head. I get up and shuffle over to the calendar

Hans pinned up. A yellow Post-it note has been stuck on one of the squares, and my hunch was right: Hans is coming over to visit this evening. And I'm supposed to ring Ture tomorrow.

My eyes are sore, my vision hazier than usual, making it difficult to see Kalle. I blink a few times, but it makes no difference. I want to talk to him about Sixten. If I could just explain how idiotic it would be for them to take him away, I'm sure he would back me up.

Right then, I feel a warm sensation spreading across my crotch again, and I sigh.

'What's up?' Kalle asks, as he loads the food into the microwave.

I sigh again, can't bring myself to say anything. The words *I wet myself* leave a bad taste in my mouth, even though it's been happening more and more lately.

'Is something up?' Kalle repeats, turning around.

There was a lot of pee this time, and there's no missing the dark patch spreading across my trousers.

'Whoops. No bother, we can sort that out,' he says, closing the microwave door without starting it. 'Let's get you into a nappy and a fresh pair of trousers.'

I don't want to do this any more, that's what I think as I meet Kalle's eyes. I want to get up and walk away. But instead, I just nod.

*5.30 p.m.*

*Bo asleep when I arrived. Prepared his dinner: meatballs and mash with a beer. Sat down to chat for a while. Bo thinks the air is icy cold and there's only a little heat from the sun. No summer yet. Reminded him that Hans will be over later. Bo had forgotten.*

*Johanna*

YOUR BELLY is so big, but you get on to the bike with such ease. Juice and buns in the basket. The dress you're wearing is one you've borrowed from your younger sister, and it looks like a sheet folded double. I'm finding it hard to see anything but your bump; my eye keeps being drawn back to it. We cruise down the gravel track, and you tell me that your sister has also saved some clothes for our little one. It could happen any day now, that's what almost everyone says. It's on my mind when I leave for the sawmill each morning, the fact that I might be a father by the time I get home.

We roll into your older sister's yard, and as ever you go straight over to the horses, press your hand to their thick coats. I like watching you with them; you seem to go so well together, and you move so naturally around them. I like to think that horses are to you what dogs are to me. Personally, I find them frightening, and I get the feeling that they can sense my fear the minute I wheel my way on to the farm. They behave differently around me than you, but then again you grew up with them and know how to talk to them. Someone like me could never understand that.

I lower the kickstand and then pause, watching you for a moment. Whenever my mind starts to wander at night, it's thoughts of you that calm me down. You're going to be such a natural with the baby, because you have what I lack. You know what you're doing, having looked after your younger siblings, nieces and nephews.

'Can you grab the buns?' you shout over to me, as you make your way towards the house.

You always bake something sweet each time we visit your sisters and parents. The buns taste so damn good, much better than Mother's. You got up earlier than usual this morning to make them before we set off.

As I turn to get the bag from the basket, a noise cuts through the air. A shrill, ringing sound. Confused, I look all around. Everything's hazy, and I'm having trouble seeing, but after a moment or two I realize I'm back on the daybed in the kitchen.

The sound starts again, a piercingly loud ring. I fumble towards the kitchen table and eventually manage to find my mobile phone. The name HANS fills the screen. I press the green button.

'Hello, Bo Andersson speaking,' I say, trying to swallow the phlegm in my throat. It always builds up while I'm sleeping.

'Hi, Dad. Were you asleep?'

I struggle to sit up, coughing and spitting into the cup on the table. Hans is quiet on the other end of the line.

'Might've been,' I say, the vision of a heavily pregnant you still fresh in my mind.

'Listen, things are a bit hectic here, so I won't have time to come over this evening.'

The company keeps him so busy, but he still comes to see me several times a week. He wants to make sure the carers are doing everything they're meant to, that there's food in the fridge and that the bin is down by the road. Some weeks he takes it down there even though it's only half full. I think that's a waste – it costs seventy-five kronor to have it emptied – but Hans says it doesn't matter.

'I thought I'd be able to leave a bit earlier today, but there are so many people on holiday at the moment and I'm swamped,' he continues, before I have time to say anything.

He sounds stressed, and I never know what to say when he gets like this. All this stress business, being burnt out or whatever it's called, I just don't understand it. He ran out of steam, as you put it, a few years back. Spent weeks holed up in his apartment with the curtains drawn. You took the spare key and went over there to cook and clean for him. I tagged along a few times, tried to get him to talk to me, but he barely said a word. I didn't know what to do.

Why doesn't he just work less? If it's really so stressful, that is. He says a lot of people at his company get burnt out like that, but I spent forty-seven years at the sawmill and it never happened to a single person. That was real hard work, so I don't know what they're doing wrong these days. Why don't you adjust the schedule, I want to ask, but he'd only get annoyed. So I hold my tongue, keep my questions to myself.

'You can always come another day,' I say, rubbing my face.

'Yeah, that's true. We need to talk about Sixten.'

I can't bring myself to respond. My hand is on Sixten's back, moving up and down as he sleeps soundly.

'OK, then let's do that,' Hans says after a brief pause.

'Let's do that.'

'Bye, then.'

'Bye,' I say.

There is a click as he hangs up, and I lower the phone to the kitchen table. I'm so angry about what he wants to do with Sixten, what he wants to put us through, but I also have a lingering sense of having done something wrong. Despite everything, I wish there was something I could say to help Hans. To make him realize he can stop stressing. Maybe he would stop thinking about Sixten if he just relaxed a little. But I don't know what I can do about his restlessness.

'You don't usually have this much to get off your chest,' Ture told me the last time we spoke, when I asked whether he thought I had something to do with all this stress business. Whether it was my fault. On the radio, they said that a person's childhood can leave deep marks.

'That's just how the brain works. You know, it latches on to things, gets itself all worked up and can't switch off.'

I nodded, because Ture probably knows plenty about that sort of thing, has had all kinds of jobs where that seemed to be the case.

'But it's not your fault. You shouldn't go around blaming yourself,' he continued, slurping as he took a sip of coffee.

His words touched me. There was just something about the way he said it that convinced me it was true.

'You're the opposite,' he observed. 'That type of stress doesn't affect people like you.'

I didn't ask him what he meant at the time – we started talking about something else – but now I'm wondering: people like me? What kind of person am I?

It's classic Ture to say something like that, analysing or whatever it's called. His imagination takes him all over the place, and sometimes he just makes things up.

Still, it doesn't bother me. If anything, it's the reason we became friends.

I'd been working at the mill in Hissmofors for nine years when Ture showed up. He got one of the new engineering jobs, but it didn't take me long to realize he wasn't like the rest of the folks working upstairs. On his very first day, he came to eat lunch with the rest of us, stomping his way down the spiral staircase.

'Hello. Ture's the name, just started here,' he said, holding up a hand and scanning the room.

A couple of the old timers looked curious, but no one said anything. Ture didn't seem to care; he just sat down and continued to chatter.

I'd never known a man with so much to say. Someone had told me he was local, but he sounded like he came from down south. There was something cheery about the way he talked, and his chatter went on and on.

'It just can't be natural to live somewhere as cold as this,' Ture said to no one at all. 'I mean, we've barely got any hair on us.'

He shook his head as he took a big bite of his sandwich.

I couldn't help myself; I burst out laughing. The man sitting opposite Ture looked so confused, it made the situation even funnier.

Ture leaned forward and peered in my direction.

'Who's the happy chappy over here, then?' he asked, raising his voice to overpower the murmur of the lunchroom.

I was still laughing, wondering who the hell this clown could be. Opposite me, Åkesson snorted. Ture grinned, and after a moment or two I managed to compose myself and hold up a hand.

'Hello, Ture. Bo's the name.'

He nodded but didn't speak. Åkesson laughed again, then grabbed my lunchbox to see what I'd brought to eat. I reached across the table to see what his wife had made for him. He was always complaining about her food, but I thought it looked good. Meat and beans. When I turned back in Ture's direction, he was absorbed by whatever the man next to him was saying.

At the end of that day, as I was walking back to my bike with weary arms, I felt a hand on my shoulder.

'It's Bo, right?'

I turned around and there he was, grinning at me. Ture's teeth were so straight and white, and his moustache so neatly trimmed into a barely noticeable strip, he looked like some American actor.

'Yup,' I said with a nod, not knowing what else to say.

'Y'know, it's been a long time since I was last around here. Grew up in Hissmofors, but I've lived in Gothenburg for a good while and I've been out on the road,' he said, doing up the top button on his coat. 'So now I'm looking for friends. You fancy coming over to my place in town sometime?'

I was so taken aback I just stared at him. You were the only one who had ever invited me over before.

'I . . .' I mumbled.

'Shall we say Sunday afternoon?'

'OK.'

And with that, Ture vanished as quickly as he had appeared.

I heard an engine start, and on the far side of the yard Ture pulled away in a shiny new Volvo Amazon. I watched the car as it sped off down the gravel track, throwing up a cloud of smoke behind it. What the hell had I got myself into?

When Sunday came round, I stared into my sparse wardrobe, thinking about the coat Ture had been wearing. It probably cost more than I'd ever blow on a single item of clothing. In the end, I took out the shirt I knew my mother would have picked.

Ture had told me he lived on the top floor of his building, and I had only just knocked twice on the door with the shiny plate with *Ture Lindman* etched into it when it flew open.

'Bo! Welcome, welcome!'

He grinned at me from the doorway and gestured to the apartment behind him. The first thought that went through my head was that he was so clean. His dark hair was gleaming. I took off my cap and made my way in.

I followed Ture as he showed me around the apartment, which was bigger than the house where my folks lived. Three tiled stoves, a WC and an electric hob. I was glad he talked so much, because I couldn't think of anything to say.

'Enough of that; let's sit down in the lounge,' he said, pointing to show me where to go. 'I bought some mazariner from Wedemarks. Go and sit down, I'll be right there.'

Ture reappeared not long after with a tray, then he poured coffee into a couple of delicate white cups.

'You ever seen the Beast, then?' he asked.

'The Beast?' I repeated, suddenly unsure. Maybe he really was mad after all.

'You know, the Storsjö Beast,' Ture explained, taking a bite of his almond tart. 'I find it so interesting. Have done ever since I was a lad. I saw it while we were out on the steamboat one Midsummer.'

Ture pushed the remaining mazarin towards my cup.

'Don't be shy. They're fantastic.'

'Thanks,' I said, lifting it from the plate. 'I've never given the Beast much thought, to be honest.'

I took a bite of the little tart, which was so delicious it took me by surprise.

'I just don't know what they were thinking when they tried to catch it,' said Ture. He seemed genuinely perplexed, even a little irritated. 'Why would anyone want to hurt it? I mean, it's never done us any harm, you know?'

He went on, telling me about all the different times he thought he had caught sight of the mysterious creature, and I found myself thinking that it was a little like being a child again, when Mother told me fairy tales about trolls in the forest. It gave me a comforting feeling deep in the pit of my stomach, and for a moment I forgot where I was.

None of my other friends from the mill were anything like Ture. There was just something about him that meant I didn't have to try too hard, in the same way that I'd never needed to put on any airs around you.

Sixten whimpers and I stroke his speckled grey head, my hand finding its way into his dreams. He wakes up and stretches. Yawns and opens his eyes, meeting mine. I can't remember when we last went out, but I can tell that he needs to pee.

I stagger out into the hallway with Sixten hot on my heels. Loop his collar over his head and straighten the little metal tag with his name and details on it. The one you and Hans ordered online when he was still a pup.

'Just in case he runs off into the woods,' you'd said, and I agreed.

I open the door for him, but as ever he waits for me to head out myself before he runs off. Always refuses to do his business unless I follow him over to the trees.

As I push my feet into my boots, I get the feeling that something special is supposed to happen today, and I go back through to the kitchen and check the calendar. Sure enough: Hans is coming over after work. And I'll call Ture tomorrow.

*9.35 p.m.*

*Hot chocolate and a sandwich for Bo, who is already tucked up in bed. Good night.*

*Johanna*

# Monday
## 22 May

*9 a.m.*

*Bo up and about, asleep in armchair when I arrived.
Wanted trout for breakfast, prepared a can of fish balls.
Given medicine and eyedrops. Reminded him that Hans
will be stopping by later.*

*Ingrid*

THE PHLEGM creeps higher and higher in my throat. I can't find anything to spit into at the kitchen table, so I get up to go to the bathroom.

The gaping toilet looms large as I lean forward and spit as hard as I can, watching as the gob of yellow mucus lands in the water, creating small ripples. The toilet bowl is stained, which makes it look filthy. I've scrubbed and scrubbed, but the marks just won't budge. Other than that, the porcelain is gleaming – it was cleaning day yesterday. Things got grubbier and grubbier after you moved to Brunkullagården, but all that has changed since the carers started coming over. I've told them there's no need, that I think it's too clean, but they say this is standard.

On my way back to the daybed in the kitchen, I pause by the photos you hung on the wall outside Hans's old room, where I also slept as a boy. I unhook one of the pictures of him from when he was around ten. He's proudly holding up the big perch we caught after hours spent out on the lake. The lad was happy for days afterwards, and I felt like the best father on earth. That same week, he gave a presentation about fishing at school, boasting all about me. About how good his dad was at catching fish.

You got to work smoking the fish as soon as we got home, and I sat and listened as Hans told you about how big he thought the fish was going to be as he reeled it in. That it had been even bigger than he expected.

I was struck by how powerful my emotions were that day, can still remember how it felt as I trace a finger over the image. How surprised I was that a fishing trip and a simple perch dinner could feel so good.

I take the picture through to the kitchen so that I can show it to Hans later, ask him if he remembers. But as I set it on the table, Sixten jumps down from the daybed and trots over to me. He presses his head against my leg. I look down at him, hesitate for a moment, then take the picture back through to the hallway and hang it up on its nail.

12.10 p.m.

Bo fast asleep on daybed when I arrive. Heated some
pancakes with jam and cream and woke him. Speech
a little slurred, hard to make out what he's saying. Told
him that lunch was ready and left the pancakes for him.
Wanted me to light a fire, but I don't dare in case there's
an accident.

Marie

I WAKE to silence. My eyes drift around the room, focusing on the light filtering in through the kitchen window. The fire has died down, and the clock has stopped, but I manage to sit up on the daybed and get the latter going again. There's something comforting about knowing that Mother and her parents all napped to the same ticking sound.

You thought it was ugly, so gaudy and awful, but you let me keep it all the same, just like I let you keep your rag rugs.

I seem to have nodded off in front of my lunch, and the pancakes before me are cold. I open the log book to see who left them there. Marie, one of the temps. That'll be why I forgot who she was; all these new faces rarely stick in my mind. I take a bite but quickly spit it out again. The pancake feels slimy in my mouth, like I'm chewing on an earthworm.

The embers are still glowing in the stove, but the temp has forgotten to add more logs before she left. I get up to try to stoke some life into it, but my head spins so much that I have to stand still for a moment, gripping the table and watching Sixten as he raises his head. He looks like he's thinking.

When I eventually manage to shuffle over to the stove, I realize that we're out of wood. I turn back to look at Sixten and briefly debate re-heating the cold pancakes, but decide to go out and fetch some logs instead.

*

Standing on the porch, I breathe in the crisp May air. The last
of the snow only melted a few days ago, and it strikes me that it
might have been the last snow I ever see. That I might never feel
the temperature dip below zero again.

My walking frame is just outside the door, and I consider
taking it over to the woodshed with me, but the last few metres
always prove tricky; it's easier just to use the wall to steady myself.

The dog pen is completely overgrown, but it's been years since
I last kept any dogs in there. The gravel inside it is hidden beneath
a thin layer of withered rosebay willowherb, and before long new
purple flowers will be in bloom. There are fewer trees there, which
gave the dogs a good view over the clearing.

Something rustles in one of the treetops, and Sixten pricks up
his ears. A squirrel darts down the trunk of a pine a little further
away, and he hurls himself after it, but doesn't make it in time; the
squirrel has already bolted up the next tree.

I've never been worried about him hurting any wild animals –
he's never been quick enough. Still, that doesn't bother him,
because it's the hunt he enjoys.

Sixten has never needed to be kept in the pen, has never been
left alone for long periods of time, because I've been at home ever
since we got him. And unlike most other people round here, I've
always let my elkhounds live indoors. The only times I used to
shut them in the pen was when I was at work. Having them howl
like banshees is no good for anyone.

I walk down the driveway and glance over at the vegetable
patch in front of the house. My mother took her time working out
exactly where to dig the beds, and most of the crops get plenty of
sun during the summer. You were excited when I first showed you
her little patch, and that made me happy. I hoped it would mean
you'd feel at home here. Just like her, you rotated between crops on
a four-year schedule. Cabbage after beans after spuds after beets.

I feel a sudden gust of wind and tug up the zip on my woollen
sweater.

'It's lucky we've got the woods,' you always used to say when it blew a gale. Unlike the lower part of the village, which is surrounded by open fields and meadows, we had the protective barrier of the pines and spruces behind the house.

I scratch my stubbly chin and shake my head. Sixten is sniffing about at the edge of the vegetable patch. Any trace of all the hard work you put in there is long gone, and the weeds have taken over. The small humps in the soil are the only sign of what this place once was.

You used to plant your young cabbages out in May, after weeks of fussing over them. The little ones, you called them, with such fondness that I realized there must be something extra special about them. Not like the beets, which you planted straight into the ground.

I feel an ache in my chest, and I close my eyes for a moment.

'She's not going to get better, you know,' Hans had snapped, when he found me out here late one evening the first summer after you'd moved. Hunched over the beds, tearing up dandelions at random.

'Like hell,' I barked, throwing my gloves down on the ground even though I knew he was right.

The two of you were always so close that I knew it upset him to see you in such a bad way, but I couldn't bring myself to tell him that. To say that I knew he was sad too.

I keep going down the drive now, until the neighbours' house comes into view. Haven't heard a peep out of them since the divorce. It's still early in the year, but their blackcurrant bushes have far more flowers than ours, which are hanging low and heavy.

When I reach the machines, I straighten the heavy tarpaulin covering the splitter and the cutter. The wind tugs it loose from time to time. Both have stood unused for years now, and I re-tie the rope to hold the tarp in place. It's a shame to see such quality kit going to waste, but Hans has forbidden me from using them, claims they're too dangerous. He buys ready-chopped logs in bulk instead.

'That's just how it is,' he says, as though I didn't spend half a century working with machines just like these.

I know he finds the cutter unwieldly, the blade terrifying. Until his teens, he used to help me split and stack the wood, but he never wanted to work the cutter, and you told me not to pressure him.

I turn around and start making my way over to the woodshed, watching out for any patches of ice that might still be lurking. The crone from the house around the bend has been over with her snowblower after every shower this winter. Hans refuses to tell me how much he pays her, but I'm sure he must be giving her something. He knows I think she's greedy, that she wants paying for one thing after another, but you went over to help that mother of hers every bloody week, and you never asked for a penny.

I pass the trail down the slope where I used to run with Buster whenever my old man lost his temper – like the time with the mouse. I can't have been much older than eight or nine. Most of the traps we used killed them instantly, traditional rat traps that broke their backs, but with a few of them you put a bit of food into a little cage instead. When the mouse went inside, the door snapped shut, trapping it.

'Go on, then,' he'd said as he thrust the spade into my hand and shoved me away. He expected me to end its life, but when I saw the little mouse darting around the cage, I just couldn't do it. Something about its tiny paws made my body refuse. I threw the spade on to a heap of earth and opened the trap. Freed the mouse. Its little legs moved as fast as they could as it darted down the slope towards the woods. In my imagination, it had a family waiting for it somewhere, maybe even a couple of friends.

His hand came out of nowhere, and the smack made my vision go dark.

'What in God's name d'you think you're doing?' he said, gripping the neck of my shirt.

I blinked to make my eyes focus.

'Sorry,' I stuttered.

He let go and pushed me away, making me lose my balance so that I fell on my backside. My cheek was stinging and I was on the verge of tears, but I tried my best to hold it together. Whenever I cried, his eyes would flash.

He picked up the empty trap.

'What's the use in me catching the little bastards if you're just going to let 'em go, eh?' he shouted, spraying me with saliva.

Out of sheer habit, I ran, even though he wasn't coming after me. I did the same every time he flared up like that. The darkness in his eyes gave me the energy I needed to run fast and far. I grabbed Buster and raced down the slope, across the meadow, not stopping until I came to the old road to Vråkäng. Only then did I slow down and start hopping between the clumps of grass growing in the middle of the track, pretending the gravel was water.

I shake my head and go into the woodshed. Pack some logs into a paper bag from the supermarket, no more than ten, treading carefully as I turn around and start making my way back up to the house. Knut, who lives above the shop over by Bölviken, fell and broke his hip a year or so back – snapped it like a wishbone. It was barely even a fall, but the whole thing just shattered, and Ingrid says he still has trouble getting about.

'Seriously, Dad!'

I turn my head and see Hans walking towards me. Sixten runs to greet him, flattening his ears and wagging his tail as our son crouches down in front of him.

If only you knew what he wants to do with you, Sixten, I think.

Hans looks up at me, his face so like yours that I almost shudder. A sense of unease spreads through me. You'll never walk towards me like this again.

His new electric car is so quiet that I didn't hear it pull up on the driveway. So clean, too. How could we have raised the kind of man who takes his car to the automatic car-wash? He scratches Sixten behind the ear, and then straightens up and walks towards me.

'I've told you not to bring in the firewood on your own. Let me do it,' he says, practically snatching the bag out of my hand.

'I know, but I'd run out,' I say curtly, nodding down at the logs.

My throat is thick with mucus, and I manage to spit up a big gob of it. Hans seems to roll his eyes, but I'm not sure.

'What would happen if you fell and broke your leg or something out here? You could be lying there for hours with no way of calling for help.'

'Mmm, what would happen then?' I repeat irritably, toying with the idea for a moment. I wonder how long it would hurt. That kind of pain might make a person pass out pretty quickly at my age.

'You're being so childish, Dad. You do realize you make people worry, don't you? Why do you have to be so stubborn?'

He can talk. Still, I don't have the energy to argue. There's no point when he's in this sort of mood. All I can do is wait it out.

'Just take it easy, OK?' says Hans.

I shake my head, on the verge of laughter. Which of us needs to take it easy?

We stand quietly for a moment, both avoiding eye contact. If you were here, you would have said something. Filled the growing void between us.

Hans makes his way down to the woodshed and fills the bag to the brim. He's put on weight over the past few years. Maybe I should ask what he's been doing for exercise. He used to do a lot of judo. I could say something gentle and inquisitive, like you used to.

'I'll take this in,' he says, holding up the bag. I think I catch a glimpse of something regretful in his eyes before he turns around. 'Wait here, and I'll come back and help you.'

I could manage the ten metres without a problem, but I stay put like an obedient child, watching his back as he walks away. Even that is getting fat.

There are little heaps of grit everywhere, left over from the winter. Hans insists on spreading far more than he needs to. I lift my foot to kick at one of the piles, want him to know that I'm angry, but the movement makes me so unsteady I quickly lower it again.

You always kept your cool. It didn't matter how much he flew off the handle.

'Anger does nothing for morale,' you used to tell me when I said that he needed you to show more authority. That you should shout at him when he slammed the door. It irritated the hell out of me when he disrespected us, acting like he didn't appreciate everything we'd done for him.

'Morale,' I muttered, remembering my old man ranting and raving, wanting to point out that it hadn't done me any harm.

But as our son walks towards me now, I realize that you might have been right. Because it was never you he shouted at over the years; it was me. The problem is that I just can't help it, the rage. It washes over me like a tidal wave.

Now that my anger has faded, I regret wanting to kick the grit and cause a fuss. I've decided to be more conciliatory instead of angry.

'I'm going to see Mum soon. Do you want to come with me?' he asks, giving me the same look he once gave us after we found out he'd nicked a Snickers.

I don't speak, because I don't want any of this. I can't understand why he insists on visiting. It's not even *you*. It's a husk of you.

He hooks his arm through mine, and we walk back towards the doorway together. I'm struck by how sturdy he is, can't quite believe that he is both taller and broader than me. Hans only weighed six pounds when he was born; these days he's big enough to pick me up.

'I saw Marita on the way over, out on the tractor. She told me to say hello.'

I nod and picture Marita on her ancient red tractor. The heat from Hans's body brings me a sense of calm. I'm still angry with him for wanting to take control of my life, but on the other hand I never want him to let go.

'Of course we can go and see your mum,' I mumble, gripping his arm tighter.

He parks me in the armchair. People often do that nowadays, parking me in various places as though strapping me into some kind of passenger seat.

Hans unclips Sixten's lead but leaves his collar on, and Sixten hovers in the hallway, confused. He pricks his ears and stares at me.

'I'm just going out to the workshop to grab something,' Hans tells me, thrusting the local paper into my hand. 'You can read this in the meantime. It was in your mailbox.'

The door has swung shut behind him before I have time to ask for my glasses. I can't even make out the headlines without them.

What I really want to do is sleep, so I close my eyes instead of getting up to fetch them. I can almost always escape into sleep. It's the place where everything is still as it should be, where I still have a say.


'Look what I found!'

I flinch, eyelids fluttering. Hans is holding up the box of old fishing tackle, a big grin on his face.

'I have so many memories of this box,' he says with a slow shake of his head. 'Do you remember how often we used to go out together? Especially over the summer. We went down to the bridges by the ferry to the island. Do you remember?'

Of course I do. His eyes had been like dinner plates when I showed him how the equipment all worked. What he could catch with the different lures.

'Careful, they're sharp,' I'd said. 'You could hurt yourself.'

His little body was so close to mine that I could feel his hot breath as he followed my every move, watching to see what I did.

I look up at our son now. Of course I remember how proud you were every time you got a bite, I want to tell him. How he had to struggle to keep his bubbling pride in check on the way home. How he used to run up the drive and tear the door open to tell you about all the fish he'd caught.

I can't help but smile, and Hans smiles back.

But I also remember when I started going fishing on my own. When he said he didn't have time, and our trips to the water became increasingly rare.

Hans sets the box down on the kitchen table.

'I haven't been fishing in years. Why is that?' he asks without looking up.

He pulls out a chair and sits down at the table. Opens the box and lifts out the compartment inside, inspecting the colourful lures.

He gives me a quick look, and I'm worried he is about to ruin this moment, that he'll say something about Sixten, but then he turns his attention back to the lures. Trailing a finger over them, one after another.

Careful, I want to tell him, but I hold my tongue. I wish I could put a hand on his head and ruffle his thinning hair.

*6.10 p.m.*

*Hash, mashed potato and beer. Bo and I have a nice chat about the olden days. He tells me all about Buster, etc. Bo dozes off before I go, so I leave the radio on. Returned a box of fishing tackle to the shed.*

*Ingrid*

I WAKE up when Sixten stretches, pressing so hard against the backrest of the daybed that his paws push me towards the edge. If the bed were any narrower, I would probably fall off it, but there's plenty of room on this old thing. It came from Mother's childhood home, and there's space to store all sorts of things beneath the lid.

My eyes drift along the wide boards on the ceiling. The wood is discoloured, dark from all the fires that have been lit over the years, and the nails beneath the pale green paint on the walls stand out like black spots. A few years back, Hans paid Ellinor to scrub the walls in the kitchen. I didn't think there was any need, but I kept my mouth shut because Ellinor was so excited to earn a bit of money.

'The ventilation in this room is useless,' Hans said with a shake of his head. 'Just look at the state of it.'

I didn't argue, because he was right. Sometimes it can actually be quite tricky to get the fire going in the morning, but all you have to do is open the front door for a while. Give it a bit of a boost from the get-go, and it'll burn nicely.

The boards on the ceiling are long and wide, beautiful wood. My old man bought it from a family a few kilometres north of here. I wonder whether Hans will repaint them when I'm gone, or whether he'll just sell the house as it is. Because Ellinor probably isn't going to want to live here.

The wide planks, with their knots and wavy lines, remind me

of my early days at the sawmill. When, as a twelve-year-old, I joined my father at work in Hissmofors for the very first time.

I remember spending a good while waiting for him out front with my bike that morning. I'd been looking forward to that day for so long, to finally being allowed to tag along. To leaving school and really beginning my life. I'd been down to the sawmill before, of course, stacked the split-wood during the school holidays, but this was different. I was done with school for ever, ready to start working for real, like my old man and all the others.

I was itching to get going, butterflies in my stomach. It was all I could do to keep myself from taking off down the road. The buds had just begun to open on the birches, and they were so green that they made my eyes ache. The lake was perfectly still, the church spire rising up from behind the trees past the mill.

He came out at long last. Paused on the porch and stared out into the woods for a moment, as though he were waiting for something, then closed the door behind him.

'Right, let's make tracks then,' he said, swinging his leg over the crossbar of his bike and setting off towards the road.

He sped away from me on the downhill slope, and I pedalled as hard as I could to keep up. Once the road flattened out again, I cruised up alongside him. Cautiously glanced over to see what sort of mood he was in.

I wanted to ask what he thought I might end up doing that day. Whether I would be marking timber, chopping wood, or laying stickers to help dry out the boards. He was tired, often was at that time of day, so I remained quiet. Didn't want him to see that I was nervous, wanted to prove that I was man enough to handle whatever was asked of me.

When we sat down at the dinner table that evening, I felt Mother's eyes on me – more than usual. I knew she wanted me to tell her about my day, and I had to bite my tongue, because I really wanted to. About all the things I had done, about my group leader, about Father and my lunch break. But I also wanted him to speak first.

'So?' Mother asked after a while.

He stared blankly at her.

'The boy,' she said, turning to me. 'How did he get on?'

The boy, I snorted to myself, as I poked at the meat on my plate. I wasn't a boy any more.

My father took a swig of beer and fixed his eyes on me, but still he didn't speak. He remained silent for what felt like an eternity, then finally raised his glass.

'Here's to Bosse, he did a good day's work today.'

The corners of my mouth twitched so much that I couldn't help but smile, and it almost felt as if he was smiling back.

'Hello, Bosse,' one of the men at the mill had said as we parked our bikes that morning, gripping my hand so hard that it almost hurt. 'Big day today, eh?'

Some of my schoolfriends called me Bosse, but no one in my family ever had. 'I christened you Bo for a reason,' Mother always said whenever someone used that nickname. And it had stuck.

But that evening she just laughed and looked at my old man with an unfamiliar warmth in her eyes.

Something changed in that moment, and I found myself enjoying being at the table with them. My body was weary, but not in a bad way. It was as though I suddenly knew what life was all about and how I was going to approach it.

The kitchen window was open, and the cranes' trumpet-like cries found their way in to where we were sitting.

'The young un's probably trying out his wings,' said Mother, taking a sip of water.

I nodded at her, my grin growing even wider. She smiled back and sat tall, then leaned forward and doled out another helping of beetroot on to my plate.

# Pentecost Eve

*8.10 a.m.*

*Bo on the daybed when I arrived, wanted rosehip soup
and jellied veal sandwiches. Sixten needs to go out, but I
don't have time. Bo says he'll take him. Reminded him to
be careful, told him to stick to the road and not go down to
the woods.*

*Johanna*

I TAKE care where I step. Sixten is running up ahead, but he keeps stopping to make sure I'm still here. The trail is littered with debris from the squirrels' meals last autumn, and the scrub and branches have bowed so low that they're practically at one with the ground. My old man used to drag the leftover wood out here, anything he couldn't be bothered to burn.

'Takes more effort to chop it up than the heat we'd get out of it,' he'd said, pointing to the wheelbarrow full of branches.

The wood wasn't all that heavy, but I really had to focus to make sure the barrow didn't tip, because it wasn't made for a small body like mine.

'Wait,' he said, gripping my left shoulder before bending down to grab another armful of twigs. He shoved them into the barrow, making the wood snap. One day, I thought, I would be that strong too.

I pause outside the root cellar my old man built into the side of the hill. It isn't big, but there was enough space for the vegetables and the jams Mother – and later you – stored during the autumn. It's been a long time since I was last in there. Most of the root vegetables I eat now come from a freezer.

When I was a boy, our house was the only one on this edge of the village. There was nothing but fields where the other homes are now, and I used to earn a bit of money cutting grass to make hay before I started at the sawmill. My old man showed me how to sharpen the scythe, and Mother sent me off with a couple of sandwiches on my first day. I liked the work, enjoyed being outside all day, and the more I did it the better I got, swinging the scythe to cut the stalks in one fell swoop. He should see me now, I used to think. As I worked in the fields, I dreamed of buying a brand new Monark bicycle, the kind with the shiny aluminium parts. If I saved for long enough, maybe I'd be able to afford one some day.

When I got home one afternoon, my father was standing on the porch. His eyes bored into me as I walked towards him, and I realized something was up. I paused a few metres away and straightened my rucksack on my shoulder. I said hello and then glanced over towards the trees, having learned from a young age that it was best not to look him in the eye.

'I'll be off to the sty, then,' I said.

He still hadn't said a word, but when I lowered my rucksack to the ground he pulled his right hand from his pocket and held it out to me.

At first I wasn't sure what his rough upturned palm meant.

'You think you can live here for free, do you?' he grunted after a moment.

The fact that I hadn't seen it coming might be what stoked my anger that day; it just felt so unfair. I was the one who'd earned the money from Evertsson, the one who'd spent the day toiling in the fields. I don't know where I found the nerve, but I raised my head and met his eye as I reached into my pocket and gripped the coins.

Before I could run away, he grabbed my shoulders and started shaking my body, even though I was almost as tall as him.

'You deaf or something? Hand it over!'

A fleck of saliva hit my cheek, and I scrunched up my face. His grip was so strong that it made my tired arms ache. Suddenly he let go and I took an unsteady step back. On any other day, I would have bolted, fled to the meadow in the woods, but I stood my ground. I knew it would only annoy him even more, but I wasn't afraid. If anything, my anger kept growing.

He took a step towards me, and I slowly backed away, saw the darkness in his eyes deepen.

'Come on, Lars-Erik. That's enough now, OK?'

We flinched, both of us. Hadn't noticed that Mother had opened the kitchen window and was watching us.

'The lad's had a long day; he's worked hard.'

Her upper body was hanging out of the frame, her forehead creased with worry, the way it always was when she thought he had crossed the line.

Not even Mother's presence was enough to settle my anger, but the old man backed up slightly and stared at me, as though I was the one who had spoken. I gritted my teeth and watched as the darkness in his eyes faded. He reached up to rub his forehead and grunted, then thrust his hand out again. But this time there was uncertainty in the movement.

His hesitation made me pause, and I stood very still. Then I saw the darkness returning, so I took out a couple of coins and put them in his hand.

'Can you help me in the sty, Bo?' Mother asked, just as I was about to take out another.

I turned my head towards the window where she had been standing, then back to him. Gripped the last few coins so tightly that it made my hand ache. Knew he realized I had been paid more.

'That's it,' I said, feeling both exhilarated and afraid.

We stood in silence until Mother came out. He slowly cracked his neck, and it felt as if the entire world had been turned upside down, as if I was finally one rung above him.

I quickly left and followed Mother over to the sty. Found myself grinning.

A branch breaks deeper in the woods, and Sixten shoves his snout into a rotten trunk. His tail is wagging languidly from side to side, and for a moment I worry he might have caught a mouse that hasn't quite woken from its winter slumber.

I turn right when I reach the wooded meadow, pausing by the

stream as Sixten worms his way through the thick vegetation. The leaves haven't unfurled yet, and the grass is barely up, but it's still a struggle for him, the aspen and spruce branches clawing at his nose. When he eventually reaches the flowing water, he spends a moment sniffing at the bank before jumping over to the trail on the other side.

Sometimes I like to pretend that I'm him, that I can feel the ground beneath his paws and his muscles working – especially when he heads out into the meadow. Every part of his body working in harmony to carry him forward at incredible speed.

I stumble as I reach the felled area, but I manage to regain my balance just in time. The weakness hits me without warning, and I sit down on a stump by the edge of the trees and lean back against the trunk behind me. I've come down here with every puppy I've ever had, the perfect distance for a little one who can't manage to walk too far.

The water from the melting snow has collected in the hollows on the trail, and I know that it often floods down here in spring. You used to love these deep pools of water, stomping through them in your boots as if to make sure they really were watertight.

I squint towards the overgrown trail among the trees. If I didn't know it was there, I wouldn't be able to see it. The long grass and the lingonberry bushes have hidden what was part of my everyday life as a lad. It must be decades since the trail was last used. I couldn't bring myself to walk it again, not after what my old man did. For weeks, I found it hard even to set foot in the woods. The trees, the ants and the swirling brook: all of it reminded me of his cruelty.

I feel an ache in my chest and look away. Don't want to remember that sort of thing.

With swollen fingers, I reach into my pocket and pull out a sweet bun. Hans buys a big bag of them from ICA Maxi whenever he goes shopping, but they're nothing compared to your cardamom buns. I take a bite. It's tricky to chew, but the saliva in my mouth helps to break up the mouthful after a while.

Sixten pauses and turns his attention to me.

'You can relax, I'm just having a rest.'

He trots over and lowers his head to my knee. Waits for me to give him a scratch.

Right then, another branch breaks somewhere deeper among the trees. I don't have time to grab Sixten's collar before his head snaps back, ears pricked. Two large elk dart across the clearing, and he takes off after them.

'Sixten!' I manage to shout, too knackered for anything else. I know there's no point, either.

He won't attack them, so there probably isn't any reason to worry. I remind myself that it's the chase he enjoys, being able to run after them.

Bright spots appear before my eyes when I try to get up, and I have to sit down again. I squint over to the trees on the far side of the clearing, where the two elk disappeared, along with Sixten hot on their heels. I know he could just as easily reappear from behind me, but it feels like I can't take my eyes off the spot where he vanished.

I tip my head back against the trunk and let my eyes drift up to the hunting tower by the edge of the trees. It must be a long time since anyone went up there, and I find myself wondering whether it's still in use. I know you thought I was a wimp for not being able to shoot an animal, but it was as though I could feel their fear pulsing through me, and every time I wrapped my finger around the trigger, something seemed to shift inside me. Almost as though I were aiming at myself.

I told you I didn't want to go hunting because it was boring. I told my old man the same, but he just snorted. In the end, I stopped saying anything when he said I should be joining them each autumn. You knew as well as he did that it wasn't true, but you never said a word, even though you would have liked me to bring home some game, like your father had.

Little by little, my strength returns, and I open my eyes. They're immediately drawn back to the clearing, but there is no sign of Sixten.

The strength seems to have returned to my legs, and I'm disappointed. It might sound ridiculous, but sometimes when the weakness and dizziness hit me like that, I find myself hoping that my time is up. On the other hand, I'm relieved, because I'm meant to call Ture today. I push back my shirt sleeve to check the time and realize I should probably be heading home.

I know he can't hear me, that he'll be long gone by now, but I still shout Sixten's name as loud as I can.

As I pass the stream, I get tired again. Sit down to rest on the 'little stone', as Hans called it. I helped him build a den here on his eighth birthday. He'd asked for wood and materials to build a fort, and we spent a whole day trying to get it just right. We went home to eat the lunch you'd made, but the minute he'd wolfed down the last mouthful, he ran back here again.

I turn around at regular intervals to shout and wait, listening for the sound of Sixten's paws hitting the ground, but there is no sign of him, so I keep going. With a bit of luck, he'll have gone west, over towards Marita's place, and someone will spot him. I try not to think about the fact that they can lash out sometimes, the elk, when they get scared or annoyed. Akesson's bitch almost died after a hoof to the head.

The minute I get home, I go inside and grab Sixten's food bowl. Take it out on to the porch and hit it against the bricks, making the metal sing. That used to help whenever he ran off as a puppy; today the sound just ebbs away without result.

Weariness washes over me again, and I take off my shoes and coat and go through to the kitchen. Write SIXTEN! on a scrap of paper and set the egg timer for fifteen minutes. Barely have time to put it down on the table before I've dozed off to the soft ticking of the clock.

THE SHRILL sound of the egg timer cuts through my sleep and drags me back to the kitchen. It takes me a moment to remember where I am and what is happening. My body puts up a fight, clinging on, desperate not to wake.

I force myself to sit up. Rub my face and take a sip of water from the glass in front of me. It tastes stale.

Right then, I spot the note on the table. SIXTEN! I get up far too quickly, and everything goes black, making me slump back on to the daybed. I sit still for a moment, then try again, slower this time.

After pushing my feet into my boots, I open the front door. Sometimes he's waiting for me there, but the paving stones outside are deserted.

'Sixten!' I shout, pulling the door to behind me.

I do a loop of the house to make sure he isn't in your old compost heap, but there is no sign of him. As I'm doing that, I remember that I'm supposed to ring Ture, and I start shuffling back towards the door. I tell myself that Sixten is still just following a scent, that he'll be back soon.

I flop on to the daybed, put on my glasses and grab my phone. There are so many symbols and characters on it that it makes my head spin, though Hans helped me change the settings so that the text and numbers are extra-large.

The list of called contacts switches between Ture, Hans and Ellinor, and I press the green button and *Ture*. The minute the call goes through, I switch to loudspeaker and lower the phone to my belly. Ture is expecting me to ring, but it always takes him a while to pick up. Sometimes the answerphone even cuts in, but he always calls back after a minute or two.

'Bo, my friend.'

I feel a rush of warmth. Ture's voice is clearer than mine. He doesn't have any trouble with phlegm in his throat like I do.

'Ture, Ture,' I chuckle. 'You were quick today.'

Just hearing his voice helps ease my worries about Sixten.

'Yup, I'd managed to make some coffee and set the table before you rang.'

Ture often drinks coffee when we chat on the phone, always has, even when we were younger. It makes him feel like we're in a cafe, he says.

'What sweet treats have you got in store for today, then?'

'A mazarin,' he says cheerily. 'Malin said they were on offer at Hemköp, so she bought a few and put them in the freezer.'

Ture has never had to worry about money, but he still likes to be thrifty. He's always telling me where I can find the best deals in town, even though he knows I only shop at the cooperative.

Malin is his Ingrid, though on the whole we've decided that my carers seem better than Ture's. We're entitled to roughly the same level of care – they wash and feed us, clean our homes – and he and I often joke that all we have to do is open wide and follow them to the bathroom when they tell us to. At first, we used to keep track of when they came and went, and though we're both supposed to get the same amount of time in the shower and help using the toilet, they would generally spend longer at my place than his. They sometimes spend longer here than they really have time for – except for the temps like the battle-axe.

I can hear Ture nibbling on his almond tart. It sounds like a good one, and I cast a quick eye at the table to see if there is any chocolate left, but I can't see any.

You were never all that fond of Ture. That's not to say you

rejected him or anything, but when I asked why you were always so quiet when he came to visit, you said he was odd and that you couldn't wrap your head around him.

You didn't make a big deal out of it, but things always felt different when you were there. Take the first time he came to see us in Renäs. We'd just moved here from Hissmofors, and Ture had been in Gothenburg all summer. I asked you to take out a nice piece of meat, said that maybe you could make your amazing brown sauce. Hans was with your little sister for the weekend, so it was just the two of us at home.

'Why does everything have to be so nice, just for him?' you asked with your back to me, as you kneaded dough at the kitchen counter.

'We always cook a good piece of meat for guests, don't we?' I asked, my eyes on the back of your head.

'Pff,' you replied, slapping the dough down with far more force than usual.

We stood quietly for a minute or two, and I couldn't work out why you seemed so annoyed. The cool autumn nights had arrived, so I made my way over to the stove and threw another log on to the fire.

'A grown man who collects figures of mythical beasts?' you snorted after a moment, turning around and fixing your eyes on me. You were waiting for an explanation, but I had no idea what I was supposed to explain.

I shook my head and closed the stove door. I thought that collecting little china figurines and hand-carved Storsjö Beasts was a bit strange too, but it also didn't matter. Not enough to get worked up over, anyway.

'What does he even want from you?'

'What are you talking about?' I asked, though I worked it out the minute the question left my mouth. I knew there had been plenty of rumours about Ture while you were growing up in Hissmofors, but he had never tried anything with me. He was a good friend, and that was that. 'A load of rubbish, that's what that is,' I snapped.

You quickly turned around and started kneading the dough again.

I don't know what you were thinking, but I got up from where I was crouched down in front of the stove, went through to the porch and came back with a few logs. How would it look if people started listening to all the local gossip?

'Mmm,' you mumbled, so quietly that I could barely hear you. 'I just think you should be careful.'

I went back out to the porch, and pushed my feet into my boots to go outside and stack more wood. Still had a whole heap left to do, and it wouldn't be long until the snow arrived.

By the time I got back inside, you'd taken out a joint from one of last year's sows and were now knitting in your armchair. I said a quiet hello to you, but we didn't say another word about Ture.

At six o'clock on the dot the following day, Ture knocked on the door. He was always on time. I had been looking forward to seeing him, to showing off our new-old house. Ture stepped into our cramped porch, took off his hat and hung it on the rack. His thick, neat hair gleamed in the light of the bulb. We hugged, and I think he was as pleased to see me as I was him.

We went through to the kitchen to sit down, Ture on the daybed and me on one of the wooden chairs opposite. You were at the stove, finishing off the sauce. I noticed that you'd made an effort to set the table nicely, with folded napkins instead of the usual kitchen roll. Your parents' cutlery, too.

'Come on then, tell us all about Gothenburg,' I said, opening a bottle of beer and holding it out to him. 'What did you get up to?'

'A lot of walking along the docks, watching the ships being loaded and unloaded,' he said, taking the bottle. 'You would like it there. It's incredible how big they are.'

He took a swig of beer, leaned back and lowered the bottle to his lap. I loved listening to Ture's stories of Gothenburg. They gave me a glimpse into a different world, of places and people I'd never seen.

'And my god, I ate so much fish,' he said with a grin. 'You should see their fish markets, Fredrika.'

'Oh?' you mumbled, adding a spoonful of fresh lingonberry jam to the sauce. 'Where did you stay?'

Ture shrugged. 'Just with a cousin,' he said, setting his bottle down on the table and gazing out through the window. 'Great view you've got here. Having Oviksfjällen on the horizon definitely beats the sea.'

I nodded, though I had never seen the sea myself. Thought I could see something downcast in his eyes.

'OK, help yourselves,' you said, setting the sauce jug down on the table and handing Ture a spoon for the spuds.

I carved the meat and dished it up on to the three plates. The cream in the sauce made it extra delicious.

'I didn't know you had a cousin in Gothenburg,' I said after a moment. 'Has he never been up to visit you?'

'Nah, there's nothing for him here,' said Ture, wiping his mouth with the napkin and turning to you. 'This is delicious, Fredrika. You really know how to cook.'

You smiled a little, but didn't speak.

'So, I hear Hans is back at school?' Ture continued, lowering his cutlery.

School was something he brought up from time to time, how important it was for Hans to get an education. I always thought it was a bit much; Hans was only a lad. Having an education was all well and good, but a person could get by without – just look at me: never went without work a day in my life. Still, Ture knew all about that sort of thing, so I left him to it. Hans seemed to enjoy school, too.

I coated a piece of meat in sauce and said that he had a new teacher, from over in Vilhelmina.

'You don't fancy having kids of your own?' you asked Ture without warning.

You had barely said a word so far, and Ture and I both jumped. Eyebrows raised, I tried to catch your eye as Ture cut into his pork. You weren't normally one for asking questions.

'I work so much, you know?' Ture said after a pause. He picked up his beer, but didn't drink.

'That's never stopped other men.'

I was so stunned I couldn't manage a single word. You knew perfectly well that Ture wasn't involved with any women. What had got into you?

'Well, as you know, Fredrika, I'm not married,' he said, lowering the bottle again.

You nodded and sipped your milk. I still couldn't bring myself to speak, and the three of us were silent around the table.

After that day, Ture and I generally met one-on-one. He still came over from time to time, for dinner or coffee, and you were never rude or anything like that, but it always felt different when you were around. I didn't mind going into town to see him instead, or over to his place.

On the other end of the line, Ture clears his throat.

'So, how's Sixten doing?' he asks.

'He's fine, but he ran off this morning. Chasing a couple of elk.'

'Uff. It's not the first time that's happened though, is it?'

'No . . .' I say, reminding myself that he was missing for half a day last autumn, in the middle of the annual elk hunt. Nejla brought him home that afternoon, said that he'd found him over by Ranåsen.

'I'm sure he'll be back soon,' Ture reassures me.

I nod, though I also remember Greta and Stisse's foxhound, which ran straight into a sharp branch. Punctured a lung and had to be put down.

*Pull yourself together.* I shake my head.

'Hans has banned me from taking him into the woods,' I say, clearing my throat. 'He wants him to go and live somewhere else.'

I feel my throat tighten as the words leave my mouth.

'Still, huh?' Ture mutters. 'What's he so scared of?'

'That I'll fall and break a leg,' I say.

That's Ingrid's explanation, at least.

'But so could a fifty-seven-year-old!' Ture grunts. 'You should be happy you don't live in town. There's no way they'd be willing to walk a dog if you were there. No chance.'

Out of nowhere, I feel weary and regret bringing up Hans's plans to take Sixten away. It always makes me so glum. Though at the same time, it's comforting to talk to someone who listens, who I know wishes me well.

'Ingrid will sort it out, you'll see,' Ture says after a moment.

I nod, my eyes on Sixten's empty water bowl.

Neither of us speaks for a moment. Ture slurps his coffee, and I hear the wall clock he inherited from his parents ticking in the background. Mine is much quieter than his.

It's been a long time since we were last able to meet, but I can picture his movements so clearly: his hand shaking as he lifts his floral coffee cup, no bigger than half a tennis ball. To avoid spilling it and burning himself, he never fills it more than halfway.

I know he enjoys watching TV, so I ask whether he's seen anything good lately. I can never get into the series he likes, but I like listening to Ture talk about them.

'How's Ellinor doing? Have you heard from her since the last time we spoke?'

I can't remember when I last talked to our granddaughter, whether it was before or after my most recent call with Ture. Time and memory merge together in a sludge, and there are days when my first few years with you feel closer than last week. Old teachers and classmates come to visit, and memories I've long repressed come flooding back.

Sometimes I can tell from Hans's face that I've said something crazy, something that belongs in another era. He gets a sad look in his eyes and he stops talking. Either that or he changes the subject. It always makes me feel so stupid, and I want to explain, but he doesn't want to listen.

'I spoke to her a few days ago,' I say, though I'm not at all sure that's true. Then again, Ture's memory is in about the same state as mine, so if I tell the same story twice it won't make much difference.

'Any gossip?'

I laugh so hard that my phone bounces up and down on my belly, and I try to think of something Ellinor might have said that Ture would enjoy.

He has always loved gossip – especially village gossip, as he calls it. I find that side of him a bit ridiculous, but it's also funny how worked up he gets. I even exaggerate local disputes for him from time to time, just to keep him happy. Spicing up my stories so they work better over the phone.

'She's seeing two boys at the minute, and neither of them knows about the other,' I say after a moment's thought.

Ellinor has always liked telling her grandad whenever she falls in love with the whole world, as she puts it. Her stories often make me blush, but I don't think she notices.

Ture hoots with delight, and I hear the china clink as he lowers his cup to the saucer.

'I knew she took after her old Uncle Ture,' he laughs. 'Tell me more!'

*1.30 p.m.*

*Bo has a fire going. Nice and toasty inside. Sixten did
a runner this morning, but Bo says he'll be back soon
enough. Compote with milk and a liver pâté sandwich,
wolfed both down. Eyes might be a bit better.*

*Kalle*

I WAKE to a soft knocking sound, and from where I'm lying on the daybed I can see a dark figure in the doorway.

'It's just me, Dad.'

I blink a few times and manage to get my eyes to focus. It's light out. I try to sit up, but don't have the energy.

Hans kicks off his shoes and comes into the kitchen.

'I honestly don't know why you insist on sleeping on that uncomfortable old thing,' he says, shaking his head. 'You've got a nice soft bed in your room.'

The daybed is perfectly comfortable, and I sleep just fine on it, I want to say. I clear my throat and try to swallow the mucus.

Hans moves over to the counter and fills a glass of water, sets it down on the table.

The absence of Sixten's weight against my legs quickly brings me back to my senses, and I rub my face and catch sight of the home-help log book. Remember that Kalle said he had written something about Sixten.

'Dad . . .' Hans begins.

I reach across the table to close the book, don't want to give Hans grist for his mill. He'd probably blame me for Sixten running off, tell me that I'm too old to take care of him.

But my body isn't quite awake yet, and I slump back down on to my side.

Hans barges between the table and the daybed and grabs me

by the armpits, pulling me up into a sitting position. I'm impressed by how strong he is, that he can manage to lift me so easily.

I wonder how old he was when I stopped picking him up like that.

'Faster, faster,' he used to hoot as I swung him around and around.

'Listen . . .' he says, immediately trailing off again.

'What?'

He exhales slowly.

'We need to talk about Sixten.'

I turn away. It's over. He'll notice that Sixten isn't here any minute now, and he'll use that against me.

But he just stands quietly, looking down at me, and I seize my chance.

'I'm glad you stopped by,' I say in an attempt to distract him.

With one of his crooked smiles, he pulls out a chair and sits down. Seems to be willing to let me change the subject. I carefully close the log book while Hans starts flicking through my post.

He looks tired, and I forget all about Sixten for a moment. Just watch our son as he casts his eye over my bills. I want to tell him to work less, to take it easy.

He uses a finger to slice open one of the envelopes.

'I can tell it's getting warmer; your electricity bill is lower this month,' he says, putting it to one side.

I want to tell him to look after himself, to be careful, but the words twist and change in my mouth. Becoming awkward and heavy.

'Mmm, but I've been using the stove too,' I mumble, thinking back to how uncomplicated it feels to talk to Ture. With him, the words flow as freely as the streams we used to fish in.

The fire hasn't quite died down yet, but Hans gets up and adds another log, gently blowing on the embers the way I taught him. Before long, the flames start dancing around it, and he sits down again.

'How's work, then?' I ask after a moment or two.

'Fine,' he says, rubbing his face. 'I've just started a new project.'

His eyes are on the fire, his job getting between us. His strange job. If he were Prime Minister or something like that, I could probably understand why he needs to work around the clock, but at a company that hardly benefits anyone? No, that's a mystery to me.

He gets up and moves over to the counter, puts the kettle on. Takes out the cafetière and a couple of mugs. His pale shirt is tight across his chest.

It wasn't always like this. When he was a lad, conversation used to be easy; there was no shutting him up. I barely had time to stretch out my legs on the daybed after work before he'd jump up by my feet and start telling me all about his day. It didn't matter that each one was almost identical to the last; he was full of beans every single evening.

'OK, your turn now,' he would say once he was done, giving me a gentle pat on the leg.

You smiled as you coated the herring in breadcrumbs. You never said much, but every now and again you would laugh or ask one of us a question.

'What about lunch? Who did you eat lunch with?' Hans would ask, if I forgot to describe my lunch break.

Watching our son make coffee now, I feel the emotions tugging at my chest.

'I've got some mazariner in the floral tin by the pantry,' I say, though I should be trying to get him to leave as soon as possible, to prevent him from realizing that Sixten is missing. The truth is that I want him to stay, so I can ask him how things are going. How he's doing.

I want to ask if he's been to any dances lately. Ingrid tells me that people don't go out dancing any more. That they do everything on their mobiles instead. Maybe he's been dancing on his phone.

'I know, do you want one?' he asks, helping himself.

As ever, I'm not hungry, but I say yes anyway. Sweet things are the only foods that still taste more or less the way they used to.

I cast a quick glance at the jar with your scarf in it and wonder what you would say if you were here. You'd probably ask something that would make Hans smirk, and have a mazarin too.

'Mmm,' I say, lifting the little tart to my lips. It's tricky to chew, and the crumbs fall from my mouth and catch in my beard.

Hans hands me a napkin and nods. I feel ridiculous.

'Like I said the other day, I'm planning to go to Brunkulla-gården on Saturday. Do you still want to come?'

No, I don't, I think, taking a sip of my coffee.

'I know you don't really want to,' he continues. 'But we can't just abandon her there, can we?'

Abandon her? Which of us has been abandoned, I want to ask. You're not the one stuck with a lifetime's worth of memories in a body that's slowly withering away.

I shrug. Take another bite of mazarin, then lower it to the plate.

The crease between Hans's eyebrows has grown more defined over the years. When he was younger, it was barely visible, but it's now so deep that there's actually dirt caught in it.

Sixten's water bowl is empty, and I'm amazed that Hans hasn't noticed he isn't here yet.

His phone starts to buzz, and he digs it out of his pocket and hurries through to the living room.

After a short while, he is back. He sits down at the table, his eyes still on the screen.

The urge to talk some sense into him, to guide him down a different path in life, overtakes me again. But I know that would be doomed to fail. It's been decades since he listened to me as though I have anything to teach him.

'Ask him something instead of just shouting and screaming,' you told me one day after dinner. 'Listen to what he has to say for once.'

That was unusual, because you never normally had much to say about the way I raised our son. You were busy transferring leftover meatloaf into Tupperware and scraping the dish clean.

'Do I really have to listen to all that crap he spouts about business, going on and on about freedom?' I asked, hitting the table with the newspaper.

You didn't speak, just lifted the lid and peered down into the pan for a moment, counting to yourself. After that, you bent down and put the meatloaf in the fridge.

'There's enough for two days' lunches,' you said, turning around to run the hot tap in the sink.

As Hans does whatever he is doing on his phone, I realize you were right. I want to tell him that it was stupid of me to shout and scream, that I should have listened more. That I know that now.

For a moment or two, I consider telling him about Sixten. He might even help me look for him. But in the end, he'll still use it against me.

I'm about to ask if everything is OK when I feel a sudden warmth between my legs. My cheeks grow hot, and I look down. My trousers are still dry, and I'm grateful to Kalle for making me put on a nappy this morning.

There is something pained in our son's eyes. Pleading, almost.

'No, we can't just abandon her there,' I say, my voice only just holding.

He nods, and I think I catch a hint of a smile. We sit quietly, just gazing at each other for a moment, and then abruptly he gets up.

'I've got to go. We'll have to talk about Sixten next time,' he says.

Anger bubbles up inside me.

'OK?' he says, trying to catch my eye.

I lean back on the daybed and turn away from him.

*6.30 p.m.*

*Bo asleep on the daybed when I arrived. Cooked potatoes and herring, left plate on the table. No sign of Sixten, but I don't have time to call Hans. Told Bo he has to stay inside.*

*Johanna*

HE'S NEVER been gone this long before. I get up at regular intervals to check whether he is outside, but the porch is just as empty every time. In the end, I decide to leave the door open.

My mind keeps drifting back to the moment I lost Sixten in the woods. To the elk running across the clearing, their large bodies moving with ease over the stumps and bushes, him bounding along right behind them.

I'll have to call Hans to ask for help before it gets too late, because a dog can't stay out there on his own all night. Still, I've decided to eat dinner first. To give Sixten a little more time. I dish a couple of pieces of herring on to my plate. If he never comes back, Hans will have got his way.

Just as I'm about to lift the last piece of fish to my mouth, someone knocks at the door. I lower my fork and turn my head towards the porch.

Marita's voice reaches me in the kitchen.

'Hello? Anyone home?'

I clear my throat and take a sip of milk. I hear her kick off her boots and tug down the zip on her jacket.

'Come in,' I manage to splutter, as she pops her head around the door.

'Look what I spotted when I was walking Tjonne past the end of your drive,' she says, holding up a small bouquet of coltsfoot. 'I thought you could probably do with a little bit of spring in here after such a long winter.'

Marita holds out the flowers, but I almost drop them, the stalks too short for my fat fingers. She makes her way over to the sink, takes a cup from the draining rack and fills it with water.

'How's everything round here, then?' she asks, carrying it over to the table and putting the flowers in the water. She then pulls out a chair and sits down.

'I've got herring for dinner,' I say, gesturing to the jar. 'So I can't really complain.'

Maybe I should say something about Sixten.

I get up to pour her a cup of coffee, but I'm so unsteady that I have to grip the edge of the table.

'Sit, sit, I don't need anything,' she says hurriedly.

'Pah,' I say, pausing for a moment to regain my balance.

The word sounded much harsher than I meant it to, so I flash her a quick smile. I pour two cups of coffee and carry them back over to the table.

'There's sugar if you want it,' I say, pushing the yellow sugar dish we inherited from your parents towards her.

She lifts the lid and drops two lumps into her cup. Her short nails are filthy.

'What've you done with Sixten, then?' she asks, looking around the kitchen.

Something in me lets go, and I tell her about our walk. About him running off after the elk. It all just comes flooding out.

'But he's got your name and number on his collar, doesn't he?' she asks. 'And everyone knows Sixten is yours, so I'm sure someone'll be in touch soon.'

I nod, feeling slightly reassured. It was my idea to make handouts for everyone in the area, with pictures of all the local dogs. So people would know who they belonged to if they got lost.

'You haven't had any calls?'

I shake my head.

'Hang on, let me have a look on Facebook,' she says, taking out her phone.

How is that going to help her work out where Sixten could be?

'I'll post something in the Vråkäng group, too. You never know, he could have run a long way if he was following the elk.'

I nod, though I have no idea what a Vråkäng group is.

'There. Now we wait and see if anyone replies,' she says, putting her phone on the table. 'Have you been out and about much lately?'

'No, it's been a while. Hans does my shopping, so I don't have much reason to go out,' I say, sipping my coffee. It tastes burnt.

'You know the bit of land Roots subdivided? The house is almost finished now,' she says, slurping her own coffee. 'What a place. Must be about three times the size of yours.'

She shakes her head.

Roots lives across the road from Marita and owns half the woods round here. She and her husband Nejla own the other half. They live more or less in the centre of the village, in one of the oldest houses. I was at school with her parents, Rolf and Gunilla. They had a farm with lots of land, and she inherited it from them. These days, she leases the fields out to a farmer in the next village over, but takes care of the woods as well as her old man did, not leaving any areas completely free of trees nor selling off bits of it to developers.

If it wasn't for Marita coming over from time to time, I wouldn't have the foggiest idea about everything going on in the area. I've stopped asking Hans, because he's clueless and doesn't seem to care.

'I went over there with a list of useful phone numbers and some meat,' she says, flicking through the local paper on the table. 'Young couple. Probably only a matter of time before they have kids.'

I nod. Giving newcomers a phone list was my idea, the tasty welcome Marita's. We worked well together on the local residents' association, got lots done. Nejla is a reindeer herder, which means he's away for long stretches, and since the kids left home Marita's had plenty of time to spare.

'Everything people build is so big nowadays,' I say, taking another sip. 'No hound?'

'Yeah, one of those fluffy little things,' she says, pulling a face. 'I told them we normally take a picture of any new four-legged residents for the next village newsletter.'

I nod.

'How's everything going with the association?' I ask after a moment.

Marita shrugs.

'Oh, you know. It's not like it was.'

It's been a few years since I took a step back, and most of the new faces are recent arrivals.

'They're all so busy, you know? Never have much time.'

I lower my cup and study Marita.

'They want the meetings to be over so damn fast that there's barely enough time to eat a biscuit,' she says with a shake of her head.

'Makes you wonder why they're in such a rush.'

'Mmm.'

She has another mouthful of coffee, and we sit quietly for a while. Hans is exactly the same, always running around without any real idea of where he's going. Young folks today just aren't right; they race about like they've only got a week left to live.

If Sixten were here, I'm sure he would be by Marita's side. Head in her lap, letting her scratch his neck.

'Åkesson's daughter, over by the dip, she's having an extension built. Space for three cars, apparently,' she says, eyebrow raised.

'Oh yeah? Does that mean she's moving back?'

'No, I think they're staying put down there. Planning to come up over the summer, maybe. Three cars, though?' she repeats.

I feel the urge to laugh.

'You've got three bloody tractors,' I tell her. I'm just about to lift my cup again when I have a coughing fit.

Marita laughs, gets up and moves around the table. Thumps me between the shoulder blades to help dislodge the phlegm.

'Tractors are different,' she mutters.

Right then, her phone pings. She jabs at it and presses one of the colourful blobs.

'He's run all the way over to upper Vråkäng, the little bugger.'

'Sixten? Have you found him?' A wave of relief washes over me, and I can't help but grin.

Marita grins back, nodding as her thumbs dance across the screen.

'They say they tried calling the number on his collar.'

'Well, no one's called me,' I say with a frown. 'There's always something wrong with these damn phones.'

'Is this it?' she asks, holding up my mobile.

I nod.

'You've got five missed calls,' she tells me, shaking her head with a smile. 'The sound is right down. Let me turn it up for you.'

Marita fiddles with my phone, and I can't stop beaming. It isn't just that Sixten has been found, it's that I managed to do it without having to ask Hans for help.

She gets up and drops her phone into her pocket.

'I'm heading into town now, so I can pick him up on my way back,' she says, tucking her chair back beneath the table. 'Thanks for the coffee. Be seeing you.'

She disappears into the porch before I have time to thank her.

I lean forward over the kitchen table and grab the log book. Cross out all mention of Sixten being missing and then slump back against the pillow with a sigh of satisfaction.


A few hours later, Marita is back. Sixten comes running in ahead of her and jumps up on to the daybed. I was already awake, so I heard her car pull up on the driveway and just lay here, waiting for his arrival.

It feels like I might explode when Sixten leaps up beside me. He digs his nose into my armpit and quickly settles down. I stroke his flank, feel the coolness of his coat.

'It was a new couple over in Vråkäng. They spotted him in the woods, got him on to a lead and took him home,' Marita says as she comes into the room, still wearing her jacket. 'Seemed nice enough. She's a psychologist from Växjö.'

I look over to where she is standing with one hand on the table. 'Thank you.'

Marita smiles, and neither of us speak.

'He's a lovely dog,' she says after a moment, her eyes on Sixten.

I can't help but feel a rush of pride.

# Saturday
## 10 June

*8.15 a.m.*

*Bo pottering about. Already eaten, just wanted tea and a sandwich. Brought in wood and picked some flowers. Bo seems a little low, says he doesn't want to go to Brunkullagården to see Fredrika. Takes his pills.*

*Ingrid*

I'M OUT in the workshop, and I know they must be here some-where. The pictures of Ellinor as a child. The light is hazy, which makes it hard to see properly, and I get annoyed that the storage boxes are packed far too tightly together, and that the majority don't have handles. I have to really work hard to hook a finger in at either side, making me all sweaty, but I refuse to give up and, in the end, I manage to get one of them out.

It's full of papers, postcards and photographs, but I know exactly which ones I'm looking for and barely even bother to glance at the others.

I get tired quickly, my body longing for the daybed. I briefly consider the chair with the sawn-off backrest left in front of the workbench at the far side of the space, but then I spot them: the snapshots of Ellinor dressed as a bee for the school play in year five. She was so proud, and so were we. In one of the pictures, she's holding my hand. We're standing by the entrance to the school in Bölviken, and her head is held high, a big grin on her face. I don't know where she got it from, that costume, but she really does look like a giant bee.

I trail a thumb over her face. Hans will be happy to see these pictures. They'll put him in a better mood, I think as I gather them up, help improve things between us. Then maybe he'll change his mind about Sixten too.

I push as hard as I can, but I can't quite get the box back into its slot. Collapse on to the chair instead. I remember sawing off the backrest so that I'd have something to stand on when I painted Hans's room.

My eyes are still bothering me, itchy and irritated, and I close them for a moment. Think about Ture and how he doesn't have an Ellinor. His family will die out with him. When his heart stops beating, that's it for his bloodline. I grip the photographs tight. In some ways, I'll live on through Ellinor. One day, she might tell her kids about you, about me. I wonder what she'll say.

I look down at the pictures. Hans was so proud when Ellinor was born that he never stopped talking about her. Every little movement she made was the most incredible thing. You barely had to ask him anything, the words just came flooding out. We looked at each other differently during that time, as though we knew something no one else knew. As though we shared something no one else had access to.

The thought leaves me feeling gloomy, wakes the familiar clawing in my chest. I remember that I'm meant to be going to Brunkullagården later, to see you. That you'll stare at me as if I'm a stranger rather than the person you're meant to be with.

One day, maybe it'll be Hans sitting here, looking down at snapshots of Ellinor's children. Maybe Ellinor will be in charge of dealing with the carers, though I have a hard time imagining Hans that old. He'll never let his hair and beard grow the way I have. He'll keep shaving and using cologne until he croaks. I scratch my chin, smile, and shake my head.

How will he react when Ellinor tells him he's no longer capable of taking care of himself? Who will he be when he stops working, when his body starts to give up the way they always do? Right then, I realize that he might end up like you, forgetting Ellinor and drifting from one day to the next, and I pull a face and shake my head. Don't want to think those thoughts.

The urge to straighten everything out hits me again. I want to make things right for Hans. My legs feel stronger now, and I get up. Make sure to take the pictures with me.

Sixten is waiting for me in the middle of the kitchen floor when I get back inside, the warm summer light filtering in through the windows, making his speckled grey coat glow. I bury my hand in the thick fur on his neck, and he grunts the way he always does when he's happy. Anger makes my hand shake, and the clawing against my ribs is back. In that moment, I have to stop stroking Sixten, that's how quickly I can lose my temper. Something in me just flares up.

I think about Sixten and I think about Hans, then I throw the pictures on to the table. If Ellinor were my daughter rather than my granddaughter, if she was the one who was in charge, everything would be far better.

She would never take Sixten away.

*9.30 a.m.*

*Have taken Dad to visit Mum at Brunkullagården. We'll eat lunch at my place afterwards. Bought more food, toilet paper and soap.*

*Hans*

I KNOW it's futile, but I put on the shirt you gave me for my eight-
ieth birthday. You won't recognize it, but maybe you'll think it
looks good all the same.

My hair is neatly slicked against my scalp, and I watch the
comb in the bathroom mirror as I pull the long grey strands into
place. When it's just been washed, my hair flops drily to the sides,
but it's greasy enough to stay put today.

My face looks thin, the skin sagging beneath my eyes, and I
regret not having asked Ingrid to help me trim my moustache
when she was here. It's so scruffy when it hangs down over my lip.
I scratch my chin. When Ellinor was younger, she always used to
say that I looked like Santa.

The pictures of her as a bee are lined up on the kitchen table so
that I won't forget them – though Hans might notice them even if
I do. He can have the shot of me and Ellinor together.

As I push my long moustache to the sides, I realize that it might
be a good idea to put the pictures in an envelope, to protect them.
I think about it for a while, know there should be some in the box
where you kept pens, stationery and tape. It's all still there.

Sixten keeps darting around my feet, and I almost trip over
him as I cross the living room and open the door to the storage
space at the back of the house. He can tell something is different
today. It's not often I get dressed up like this.

I turn on the light and scan the room for the green box.

'Hello? Dad?'

I turn around and see Hans. He's wearing a dark blue shirt and jeans.

'There you are. Why didn't you reply when I shouted?'

I don't have time to utter a single word. Sometimes it feels like everything speeds up when Hans is here, like fast-forwarding a VHS tape. Before I've had a moment to finish one thought, he's moved on.

'I get worried. You understand that, don't you?' he says with a frown. 'When you don't respond.'

I close the door and watch Hans step into the bathroom and open the cupboard above the boiler, where I keep the toilet roll.

I'm embarrassed that I still haven't managed to say a word, though at the same time I can't really remember what I'm embarrassed about, which only confuses me.

'OK then,' says Hans, closing the cupboard without taking anything out. 'Are you ready?'

Ready for what, I wonder, before he reminds me:

'We're going to see Mum today. Did you forget?'

I meet our son's eyes. The dark circles beneath them remind me of yours. Other than his mouth and chin, which you said came from me, he looks just like you. The same high forehead and rounded nose. I'm struck by how strange it is that he's a mix of us both when we were younger, as I remember us, and yet we're now strangers.

'No, I didn't forget,' I say after a moment, resolutely turning around. 'Shall we go?'

I walk straight through to the hall and push my feet into my good shoes.

Hans helps me with my seatbelt and closes the car door. It doesn't take long to drive into town nowadays, just thirty minutes or so. Before they built the bridge, back when we still had to use the ferry, it took at least three-quarters of an hour. We race by the house where your old hairdresser lived. She bred litters of fluffy white puppies that we used to laugh at. Toy dogs, we called them. That was years ago now, and the salon is long gone. Who knows, maybe she is too.

'They'll be graduating soon,' Hans says, nodding to a group of teenagers at the bus stop. 'I can't believe it's been four years since Ellinor ran out on to the steps outside the school to celebrate.'

He sighs.

I nod, though I don't really remember. I know there's a picture of her in the traditional white student cap on my fridge, but I don't remember any of the day itself.

'That was a nice day,' I lie, my thoughts drifting back to Hans's graduation.

We were so proud that we paid for half his driving licence. Blew that year's holiday fund without batting an eyelid.

He didn't tell us that he'd applied to university until the week before he left. He'd taken it easy that summer, and we knew he probably had his mind set on coming up with his own plan, but we never thought he'd move all the way to Uppsala.

No, he'd been talking about starting his own business since secondary school.

'So I can earn money and be free,' he said with a dreamy look in his eye.

I glance over at him, as he focuses on the road up ahead, and wonder just how free he feels now.

The first time he came home to visit, it didn't take us long to lock horns. He wanted to talk politics, and it was as though he held me personally responsible for everything the Social Democrats had done over the years. He sounded so irritated, throwing out fancy words he must have picked up from his professors.

'People become so passive and fail to take responsibility for their own actions in this country,' he said, as though justice and welfare were things that hampered people.

You didn't get involved until we started yelling.

'Enough!' you snapped, with such force that we were both dumbstruck. Even the dogs were surprised, and trotted over to your side.

Still, it worked, and we put politics to one side. Talked about the autumn harvest instead. He asked if you needed help with anything.

I never stood up to my old man the way Hans did with me. That just wasn't something you did. He was the one who made the decisions, and there was nothing I could say. I couldn't imagine it any other way. But Hans has never had a problem yelling all sorts of things at his father.

He slows down and turns off on to the bridge. Town stretches out in front of us, sloping down towards the shore of Storsjön. His fondness for talking back has made me lose my temper so many times, but there was also something I envied about it. The confidence he had in everything he said, the fact that he thought he had the right to stand up to me.


Hans's electric car cruises into the parking area outside Brunkulla-gården without a sound. I feel a tug in my chest, a general sense of unease spreading through me. As ever, he parks in front of the cluster of birch trees that separate the care home from the nursery school. Loosens his seatbelt and takes out his phone.

'It's daylight bloody robbery that they make you pay to park,' he mutters, as he enters his details.

Visitors could park for free when you first moved in.

I'm glad I'm not the one who has to do all this app nonsense. Can't understand why there hasn't been more of an outcry about the fact that you can't even park your car without having a mobile phone nowadays.

Ellinor and Hans bought me a pensioner-friendly phone, as they put it, a few years back. It has bigger buttons and fewer features, but I still can't wrap my head around it. Ture thinks I'm being pig-headed and whiny, but I genuinely don't see what's so interesting about all these gadgets. That's because I haven't tried, he tells me. But that isn't true. Ellinor has shown me all the things she can do on her phone, and I think it is ridiculous.

The car door opens, and Hans pops his head back inside.

'Are you coming?'

I turn to the driver's seat in surprise, hadn't noticed him get out.

With some difficulty, I swing my legs out of the footwell. It's been years since I last wore my good shoes, and the left one feels tight on my heel. I grip the handle above my seat and pull myself up. The movement makes my head spin, and I have to sit back down again.

'Hold on, I'll go and get a wheelchair.'

Before I can tell him that my walking frame is just fine, he's over by the entrance. Everything always has to happen so damn fast with him. Why is he in such a rush? Everyone is in such a bloody rush.

I lean against the seat and sag a little lower. Let my eyes rest on the sign above the doorway to the building, which looks a little like the Social Democrats' logo.

Before long, I see Hans pushing a wheelchair on the other side of the glass doors, which are still open. He speeds up to make it out before they close, but they start rolling shut and the chair gets stuck. Hans swears and reaches for the button to make the doors open again, a nurse patiently waiting behind him.


Your room here is on a long corridor, and it's obvious that the staff have made an effort to make it feel a bit less lonely and unsettling. There are paintings of scenic landscapes on the walls, armchairs and sofas dotted around. At the far end of the corridor, bright summer light filters in through a window that looks out on to the parking area, and there is a small table with a stack of magazines and an armchair off to one side. Someone is often sitting there when we visit, someone it's all got a bit too much for. You're not the only loony here.

'I don't know how they could put a dementia facility in a place like this,' Hans mutters.

He thinks that the long, drab corridors make you more anxious, but you're so far gone that I'm not sure it would make much difference where you were.

Halfway down the corridor, to the right, there is a door to the kitchen and the staff changing rooms. It's always locked. The dining room and TV room are opposite. You used to enjoy eating with the other residents when you first moved here, but these days you rarely want to leave your room.

Hans stops pushing the wheelchair and opens your pale yellow door. Beside it, there is a little wooden sign with the number fourteen in blue. Around the number, someone has painted a black vanilla orchid, the flower of Jämtland.

'That's fitting for Mum, isn't it?' Hans said the first time we visited you.

I agreed, but I also found myself thinking that there was nothing fitting about any of this.

Beneath the sign, there is a small whiteboard with *Fredrika* written in looping letters.

A waft of disinfectant and stale air hits us as Hans wheels me into your room. It smells strange here, and it feels obvious that this place has nothing to do with either you or me.

Hans takes off his thin jacket and hangs it on the coat rack to the left of the door, knocking over the shoehorn I gave you for your seventieth birthday in the process. The sound of the metal hitting the floor is ear-splitting.

'What the hell . . . who left that there?'

He picks it up and leans it against the wall in the corner instead, beside your walking shoes. You almost never wear boots now. When they take you out, it's only ever for a short stroll in the park just outside.

'Sorry, but you haven't seen a key lying around, have you?'

Suddenly you're right there, your arms hanging limply by your sides. You, who have always seemed so strong, even though you're so slight.

And although you often ask about the key, Hans and I are both surprised.

'It's us, Mum,' he says, putting a hand on your arm. As though things are going to be any different this time. As though you'll recognize us and sit down to eat the buns he brought.

Hans is convinced that our visits do you good, even though we can't see any sign of that ourselves. Who knows, maybe he's right.

I glance over at our son, who briefly holds my gaze, but I don't speak. There is something sad about him, and I just want to make everything OK.

You seem confused, then sceptical. Studying us in turn.

You're wearing a pair of grey tracksuit bottoms that look just like mine, and I guess Hans probably bought them from Intersport, too. They've paired them with one of your old blouses, and the combination looks so strange that I feel like laughing.

Then I meet your eye and feel sad, because there is none of you left in there.

'Oh, you've got visitors. That's lovely, Fredrika.'

We turn around and see a smiling woman in purple, a name badge pinned to her chest. *Lena, Assistant Nurse.*

You ignore her and glare at Hans again, your face twisted in disapproval.

'Mum? Did you just call me Mum?' You draw back from him and press a hand to the spot where Hans touched you. 'I don't like being manhandled by strangers.'

You snarl the last few words. You, who barely ever raised your voice. I was the one who lost my temper. The anger in your eyes makes me feel ashamed of all the times I snapped at you over the years.

Lena smiles at me and Hans.

'Why don't I show you where we keep the cups and plates?' she says, though we know exactly where the dining room and kitchen are.

I smile back. She seems nice, and that feels good. I want the people who are looking after you to be kind.

Hans is keen to leave, I can see it on his face. The anxiety in his eyes, the same look he used to get when he'd hurt himself as a child. Something pleading. I am his father, after all. And just like that, I understand why he insists on me tagging along whenever he comes to visit you.

'Come on,' I say, putting a swollen hand on his left leg.

He turns to me, and I realize I can't help him. He wants to get away from me as much as any of this.

He grips the handles on the wheelchair and pushes me out into the corridor behind Lena. Her face isn't familiar, but we could well have met before. Unlike you, I'm aware that my memory lets me down. I can work around it.

When we get to the kitchen, Lena says, 'It might be a good idea to wait here for a few minutes. Fredrika is so worked up. If we give her a bit of time to herself, she might calm down.'

'Thanks, Lena,' I say.

Hans smiles, but he doesn't speak. He simply takes three mugs down from the cupboard where a scrap of paper with the word CUPS on it has been taped to the door.

I'm starting to get tired, longing for my daybed, for sleep and Sixten.

When we get back to your room, you're fast asleep in the armchair by the window. Snoring the way you always did, which makes me feel warm inside. I look up at Hans, and we both smile.

You wake up when he sets the mugs of coffee down on the table beside you and takes a seat. You nod at him, almost in approval, then turn to look out of the window.

Hans has parked me right in the doorway to your room, and

the black-and-white photographs from Hissmofors that he had framed when you moved here are on the wall beside me. One of the sawmill where your father, three of your brothers and I all worked; one of Folkets Hus where we met, and another of the school you attended. We both spent six years in education, and then we had to learn from life itself. When we first met, you were working as a maid at the neighbouring farm, and helping out where you could on your big sister's farm, too. We lived in Renäs for over half a century, but you no longer remember our house there. That's why we didn't bother framing any pictures of it; it would only confuse you. The early memories from Hissmofors are still there, though, and you still remember the names of your sister's two horses rearing up in the fourth picture.

You were relieved when I said I wanted to live in Hissmofors, because everything you loved was there. Your siblings, cousins, schoolfriends. When Hans was a boy, we spent a lot of time with your family. They had large farms with lots of animals, and they needed help. It was obvious that you didn't want to leave, but you didn't say a word when I told you that we'd inherited the house in Renäs, that we finally had a place of our own. We'd been renting a tiny apartment in Hissmofors until that point.

Further along the wall, there is a large colour photograph of you, me and Hans. In it, you're helping Hans hold up a big bucket of cloudberries that we picked on the way home from Ture's cabin. I'm sitting a little further back, smiling. Ture took the photograph, and he sent it to us in the post a few weeks later.

You're still staring out through the institution's triple-glazed windows, which makes me think back to our early days in Renäs, when you used to spend so long gazing off towards Oviksfjällen in the distance. You barely said a word for weeks after we moved. I think the longing made you ill.

'I'm wondering if this might be something,' you said late one evening, once the long silence was over, setting a cutting from the newspaper in front of me.

I pushed away my dinner plate and skimmed through the text. It was an advert for a secretarial course, no prior training needed.

'Pff, you shouldn't have to work,' I said, putting the ad to one side.

We never mentioned it again.

I look up at the pictures now, and my stomach turns anxiously. I wasn't really against the idea of you working, I just didn't think it was necessary. My wage was more than enough. But with hindsight, I can see that it might have been good for you to do your own thing.

'Summer has come early this year,' you say without warning. 'We'll have to be careful with the beets, otherwise they'll go to flower.'

'Mmm,' Hans mumbles.

He used to have a couple of vegetable beds of his own when he was younger. Liked to plan what he was going to sow and imagine what the harvest would be like. He kept statistics, jotting down how many kilos of beetroot or cabbage he'd grown and working out how much that would have cost him to buy.

I force myself up out of the wheelchair and make my way into the bathroom.

'Be careful, Dad.'

'Yes, yes,' I say, closing the door behind me.

The button on my trousers is a little tricky, but I manage it in the end. The nappy is much easier. Thanks to the elastic, it's no worse than pulling a pair of underpants down; you just have to hook your thumbs under the edges.

Above the sink, there is a mirrored cabinet where you keep your toothbrush and toothpaste. Some face cream and a couple of clip-on earrings you no longer wear. You've never really been someone who wears a lot of jewellery, but the first few times Hans and I came to visit you here, they'd clipped the little gold earrings with purple stones on to your ears.

When I come back out from the bathroom, Hans is waiting for me just outside. Already in his jacket.

'We should probably head off. I think Mum needs to rest.'

'Mum? Whose mum needs to rest?' you shout from your armchair.

I hold out my arms so that Hans can help me with my jacket.

For a split second, I'm about to head back over to say good-bye to you, but instead I lower myself into the wheelchair and let Hans push me away.


I flop down on to the passenger seat with a groan. Watch Hans in the rear-view mirror as he wheels the empty chair back into the home. He looks so lonely.

I wake up as he opens the driver's door and gets in behind the wheel.

'Did you doze off?' he asks.

I think I can see a half-smile on his face, which makes me happy. I nod and blink, trying to make my eyes focus.

Our son is sitting beside me with his hands in his lap, star-ing out through the windscreen. His attention seems to be on a couple of kids playing in the distance. He gets this glum look on his face sometimes, the same one he had when he shut himself in his apartment for weeks on end.

I don't know what to do. All I want is to make everything OK, but it's often like this after we've been to see you.

In some ways, it feels as though I'm better prepared for these visits. I've managed to anchor myself in what we had before you ended up like this, but Hans hasn't. He can only see you as you are right now.

He reaches up and rubs his face, and I want to say something to ease his mind.

'It's no fun seeing her like that,' I say, squinting over at the play-ing children.

'Nope, it's not.'

He rests his forehead against the wheel for a moment. He's so big that he doesn't even have to lean all that far.

'But I'm sure it does her good to see us,' I continue, clearing my throat. 'I think it does her good somewhere deep down.'

Hans turns his head and fixes me with the same look he used to as a boy. The one that tells me we belong together.

'Do you really think so?'

'Yes, I do. She seems happy there, and that Lena woman was nice.' I take a deep breath. 'It's good that you found her a place here.' I remember how angry I was when he first brought it up. 'I really think so.'

Hans nods, and I reach up and pat him on the back.

'Come on, let's go over to your place and have something to eat.'

HANS BARGES out of the lift ahead of me and unlocks the door to his apartment. It's been a while since I was last here; he mostly just comes over to my place now. I park my walking frame in the stairwell, right by his door, and the reflector knocks against the wall with a ringing sound. Hans turns the light on, and I make my way into the cramped hallway.

The first thing I notice is a large picture of Ellinor I've never seen before.

'She gave it to me for Christmas,' he explains with a nod to the photograph. 'Kept complaining that the only pictures I had of her were from when she was little. Here.'

He hands me the shoehorn. It's long and metal, which means I don't need to bend down or struggle with my shoes. The ones at the health centre are all made from plastic, and are far too flimsy and short.

'It's from Ikea,' says Hans. 'I was actually thinking of you when I ordered it.'

I smile, my eyes still on my feet. Feel touched.

'I'll get lunch ready – I bought some mushroom soup yesterday. I'll put the coffee on, too. And I got a couple of cakes from Tages,' Hans goes on, lumbering into the kitchen; the gloominess from earlier hasn't quite shifted yet.

'Thank you kindly,' I say, hanging my jacket on a hook.

It doesn't matter how many times I tell him that I can't stand the taste of cream any more, he just keeps on buying them: the little cream cakes with fruit that I used to like.

'We need to put a bit of flesh on your bones. You're getting far too thin,' he shouts from the kitchen.

While Hans heats the soup, I go through to the living room. It's emptier than I remember it. There used to be greenery everywhere, but I can only see one dry, sad-looking plant on the windowsill by the balcony.

Everything is black, white and grey, the only hint of colour coming from the pictures changing successively on the big screen opposite the sofa. Camels in a desert, mountains, a brightly coloured bird. I wonder where he gets them from. The photograph of the camels comes back on to the screen, and I can't work out how they could have taken it from above like that. Must've been from a plane.

Right then, something nudges up against my foot, making me jump. What the hell, I think; has he got himself a cat? But when I look down, I see a black plastic machine slowly rolling away from me.

'That's Robert,' says Hans. 'My robot vacuum cleaner.'

'Your what?'

I can't quite hide my surprise, and Hans smiles.

'I've told you about it before. It does the vacuuming for me every week. Very convenient,' he says, looking so pleased with himself that all I can do is smile back. 'I actually thought about getting one for you, but I think your house might be a bit messy. You've got too much stuff sitting around, I mean.'

He takes out his phone and disappears through the doorway.

I stand still, watching the little machine for a while. Shake my head and laugh as it methodically makes its way across the bare living room floor. It isn't very big, and I wonder how often he has to empty it. Without warning, it turns around and starts trundling back towards me. I quickly get out of its way, moving over to the corner by the door into Hans's office. The room where he puts in a shift at the end of the day, as he likes to say. I think Sonja used to have her sewing machine in there.

The pictures on the walls are mostly of Ellinor as a child, but we're there too. One from your sixtieth birthday, for example. You look so happy, wearing a big hat with a ribbon that says *60 Today!* on it. Sonja gave you that. I wonder how she's doing, haven't heard a peep out of her since she left Hans. My eyes scan the rest of the pictures, and I notice that she isn't in any of them. Then again, they've been divorced for a few years now, so maybe that isn't so strange.

It must have been hard on Hans, because we didn't see much of him for a while. We kept inviting him over for dinner, but he always said he had to work, even on the weekends.

'Everyone has to eat,' I used to say, and in the end he started coming over from time to time – though mostly he just sat with his eyes on his plate, chewing quietly.

We never really asked much about it, the divorce. What was there to say? She left him, and I didn't want to stick my nose into his business. It was what it was. You thought it was because he worked too much, that Sonja got sick of it.

'Maybe she met someone else,' I said one evening, when you were feeling down over the fact that they'd filed the divorce papers.

'Nonsense, Sonja isn't like that,' you said, pursing your lips. 'She'd never.'

I shrugged, because what the hell did you know? It wouldn't have been so strange if she'd met someone else. They weren't like us, after all. We were happy together, you and me. Never fought, enjoyed each other's company. Hans and Sonja could both cause such a scene, even around other people. Like the time we went to a restaurant together, and Hans was late. Sonja gave him such an earful that the whole place could hear. He could be a stroppy so and so, too. Snapping at her for no good reason when he was in a bad mood. I know I can be pretty difficult myself, but I would never speak to you the way he spoke to Sonja.

Still, he was so low after the divorce, he really was. I tried to get him to come fishing with me, but he didn't even want to do that. You went over to take him veg from your beds from time to time, the sort of things he liked.

A couple of years after they split up, he came for dinner after work one Monday, and he seemed cheerier than usual.

'There's a dance over in Sandviken this weekend,' you said, straightening your apron as you sat down at the head of the table. You liked to sit there, to be close to the kitchen in case you needed to fetch anything.

You had mentioned it to me before he arrived, that it might be something he'd be interested in. I agreed, said that we should tell him. We both thought it was high time he moved on and met someone new. We didn't want him to be alone for ever, and thought it would do him good to have a woman around. Someone to share his days with.

Hans stopped chewing.

'Just a thought,' you said quietly. 'It's been a while now.'

I stole a glance at him, unsure of what he might say, but he was just staring down at his plate. I thought it was probably best to remain silent, to let you deal with it, because you always handled that sort of thing far better than me. But then I felt you kick my leg under the table. I flinched, but Hans didn't notice.

'Your mother is right,' I blurted out, taking a swig of my beer. You gave me a look to say that wasn't enough. 'A dance might be a nice—'

'I'm not going to meet someone new, and that's that,' Hans said, cutting me off, looking up. First at you, then me.

He fixed his eyes on us in such a way that we both knew not to push him. And so I held my tongue.

'Do you remember the horses as clearly as Mum?'

I jump. Hadn't heard Hans come back into the living room.

An image of you scraping a mare's hoof pops into my head. I always thought you looked so strong when you were working with the horses. Liked watching you from a distance, as I lay in the shade beneath the big birch. Sometimes you would shout over and tell me to make myself useful, to carry something, but more often than not you just left me to it.

'Sure, but I was never as fond of them as she was.'

Hans nods, and we stand quietly for a moment. He seems to be thinking about something, and I wonder what it could be.

He gives a small smile.

'Strange, isn't it,' he says, heading back through to the kitchen.

I assume he means it's strange what you can remember, and I agree. It's also strange how much has been lost in you. Our entire life together. Still, I like to believe there must be something left. Memories that rise to the surface in your dreams. Images flickering by from time to time, as you're looking out of the window. Then again, maybe I only feel that way because the alternative is too painful.

I turn back to the photographs, focusing on one of me pulling Ellinor in the sled. It must've been you who took it. I'm standing tall, wearing the harness. Holding a pole in one hand and a saw in the other, my eyes on the woods. Ellinor looks happy and rosy-cheeked. Probably the middle of the day, given how light it seems. Going to cut down the Christmas tree every year, that was our thing. When she was really small, we used to pop her in the sled, get her cosy with a few skins, and put our skis on. You, me and Ellinor.

'Lunch is ready!'

The aroma of mushroom hits me as I make my way into the kitchen. Hans pulls a chair out for me, and I sit down. The table and chairs were your parents'. Sonja took theirs when she left, so Hans inherited ours. We didn't need such a big table any more.

'You and Ture used to go chanterelle-picking up by his cabin, right?' he asks, as he lifts the spoon to his mouth. Blowing on the hot soup before he slurps it.

I smile and tell Hans about the time we came home with

twenty-five kilos of mushrooms. You were happy for weeks. Chanterelle soup, chanterelle sandwiches, chanterelle stew, chanterelle sauce. We couldn't get enough.

The gloominess seems to have lifted at last, and I'm struck by the fact that Hans looks happier than I've seen him in a long time.

'How is he, by the way? It's been ages since I last saw him.'

'Oh, you know. It is what it is,' I say. 'We talk on the phone quite a bit.'

Hans nods and pours us both some water.

I want to ask whether he remembers all the times we went up to Ture's cabin when he was little. Some of my very best memories are from our trips there.

'How are things at work?' I ask instead.

'There's been a lot of overtime lately, but that means things are going well,' he says.

I thought everyone agreed that people should work less nowadays, I think, as I stir my soup. That we all wanted shorter working days. But from what Hans is telling me, it sounds as if people would rather work themselves to death. Ture always says it's become a non-issue, that none of the parties really think we should have more free time.

'Uh huh, and what about the politics? How's that going?'

Hans sighs.

'It's been decades since I really did any of that.'

He unbuttons his cuffs and rolls his shirt sleeves up to his elbows.

'Oh,' I say, though I know what he's just said is true.

It was all so long ago, but it still stings. He'd come home to visit from university, and as you served the spuds he announced that he'd joined the Young Conservatives.

At first, I didn't speak. Just lowered my fork to the plate. It was November, and the snow still hadn't arrived, but it was so dark that I couldn't quite read his face. I'd known something was different from the moment he walked through the door earlier that day.

It wasn't just his clothes, a blazer and a strange shirt that looked too big for him; it was the way he moved, too. He also seemed quieter somehow, like he had something on his mind. And I don't know why, but it felt as if he was watching me.

'Don't you look handsome,' you said, as he took off his rucksack and dropped it to the floor.

He smiled at you the way he never smiled at me, and you patted him on the cheek and started making him a sandwich.

Despite all that, I was still surprised by our son's announcement at dinner that evening. All his pro-business and finance talk was one thing, but actually putting himself on the side of the conservatives? No, that was something else entirely.

'Social democracy,' he said, gesturing with such enthusiasm that his hair flopped down over his forehead. 'It's a nice idea, but it just doesn't work in the long term.'

I knew you felt the same way I did, that it was absolutely bloody crazy that we'd ended up with a son who could say something like that, but you didn't say a word. You just cut off a piece of meat, coated it in sauce and raised it to your mouth.

'We can't keep handing everything to people on a plate. We have to make them work for it,' said Hans, as though he knew a single thing about hard work.

I felt the anger building inside me and couldn't tear my eyes away from the ridiculous lock of hair hanging down over his forehead. Thick with product, stinking to high heaven.

'This is a family of workers,' I said, bringing my hand down on the table and making the cutlery jump.

You moved the candlestick a little further back.

Hans grinned at me and shook his head.

'It doesn't work that way any more.'

What doesn't, I wanted to ask, but I just snorted and took another swig of beer.

'Take a good look at this and tell me I'm not a worker,' I said, holding up my fist.

'God, you're so dramatic, Dad. I'm not denying that you're a worker. I'm just saying that a person can't be born into a particular fucking party.'

That's exactly what happens, I thought, though I held my tongue. You were still sitting with your eyes on your plate. Cutting small pieces of meat that you slowly lifted to your lips.

Right there and then, I felt ridiculous for waving my fist in the air.

'You guys just don't get it,' Hans sighed.

You gave me a look that said you agreed, and we ate the rest of the meal in silence, letting the clock tick away. The minute my plate was empty, I got to my feet and knocked back the last of the beer from my can, even though I knew you didn't like it when I did that. I whistled for the hound and went down to the meadow in the woods. Didn't go home for dessert, though I knew you would be worried.

I grab a piece of kitchen roll and look up at Hans now. He still has the same haircut, still uses the same products that make my nose sting, but his shirts are much tighter now.

I remember feeling like a failure as I sat by the meadow that day. That I must have done something wrong.

'So to answer your question, there's not much to report on the politics front,' he says, taking a sip of water.

And just like that, I'm ashamed. Why did I have to bring this up? It's like I can't help it, like I'm powerless to decide which words come out. I don't want to argue, don't want to annoy him, and yet I keep saying things I know he won't like.

We sit quietly for a while, and he spoons the last of his soup from his bowl.

'Delicious,' I say after a moment.

Hans nods. He seems weary again, and I feel an urge to pull a blanket over his sleeping body and stroke his forehead.

'Maybe we should get you back home soon?' he says. 'You look tired.'

I shrug, but there's nothing I want more than to get back to Sixten and my daybed.


Hans waits in the car as I unlock the door. I have the keys on a leather strap tied to my belt loop, so I always know where they are. I lift my hand and wave before closing the door behind me, and he slowly reverses down the drive and pulls away.

Sixten meets me in the hallway, yawning and stretching one leg at a time. He'll have been fast asleep on the daybed, with his head on my pillow.

As I make my way into the kitchen, I spot the pictures of Ellinor that I meant to give Hans. The driveway is empty, and I briefly debate taking out my phone to give him a ring and say that I've got something for him. A surprise. Then again, I don't want to bother him while he's driving, so it'll have to wait until next time. That could be a while, of course, and I don't want to leave the pictures lying on the table where I might spill food or coffee on them. I hold them in my hands for a moment, then take them through to your old bed in the bedroom instead.

There is a scrap of paper beside my phone on the kitchen table. *1.15 p.m. Took Sixten for a walk, did his business. Ingrid.* She must have come in through the back door; it's almost always unlocked. I look up at the clock on the wall. Twenty past four. He'll probably need to go out again soon.

'You'll have to wait a while, because I need to rest my eyes for a minute or two,' I tell him, patting his head and making my way over to the daybed.

*9 p.m.*

*Hot chocolate coming right up. Everything OK.*

*Kalle*

# Monday
## 19 June

*3.30 a.m.*

*Night patrol found Bo by the mailboxes. Said he urgently needed to post a letter to Fredrika, but he seemed confused and didn't understand that it's the middle of the night. Got him home safely and tucked him up on the daybed. Sixten inside.*

*Night patrol*

WE'RE ON the daybed, Sixten breathing heavily on my stomach. The carers have draped one of your old blankets over me, but I can still feel the cool summer night against my legs. I'm not sure where they found it, don't remember having seen it in years.

I haven't done anything wrong, but for some reason I still feel bad. It's so typical that the night patrol happened to be going past while I was outside. They made such a big deal of it, me posting a letter to you, and all because it was night-time. But I don't have anywhere to be in the morning, no one waiting for me, and Sixten was right there with me. Still, they went bananas.

'We'll have to start coming over here every night if you're going to carry on like this,' one of them told me, a woman I've never seen before.

Since when has it been a crime to post a letter at night, I wanted to scream, but I kept quiet. The stressed look in her eyes made me think twice. My anger suddenly felt childish and unjustified.

Lying on the daybed now, it comes surging back. It's not even bloody dark outside. Surely there's no harm in going outside on a night like this. I clear my throat and swallow the phlegm, but just as I'm about to speak up, the door swings shut. I sigh.

Sixten has curled up in his basket on the floor. He wants to sleep alone tonight; it's too warm to be up here on the daybed with me.

'Goodnight, then,' I mutter, pulling the blanket up over my stomach.

*8.10 a.m.*

*Had to wake Bo when I arrived. Gave him his medication and got him to blow into the bottle. A little whiny, but he gave in after a bit of back and forth. Porridge for breakfast. Reminded him that he's due a shower later.*

*Eva-Lena*

I SLEPT for longer than usual this morning. I normally have a cup of tea some time around half five, but today I didn't get up until the carer arrived. To make matters worse, it was that stroppy cow's shift, and she started nagging me to blow into the bottle even though I barely had the energy to sit up.

My eyes look so glum in the bathroom mirror, big, puffy bags underneath. I blink to get rid of the worst of the blurriness, clear my throat and spit. The yellow slime clings to the bowl as I turn on the tap to rinse the sink clean. I dreamed about you, that was why I wrote the letter. Stood outside for a while, gazing over to the pale pink horizon above the mountain ridge.

A year before we got married, on Midsummer's Eve, you insisted on picking flowers from the meadow across from the place we were renting in Hissmofors.

'What could be more beautiful than this?' you asked, gesturing to the sea of petals.

In all honesty, I thought you were a little loopy for wanting to pick flowers so late at night, but the look in your eye could have convinced me to do anything.

'We need to know if we're meant to be,' you said, your cheeks slightly flushed. 'Whether we should really go ahead with our plans.'

It was after midnight, but I was wide awake, listening to you sing the names of the flowers as you snapped the stalks and added them to your bouquet. You told me that you and your sisters used

to go out late at night around Midsummer, and I held your growing bouquet and couldn't think about anything else.

All that came back to me in my dream. I got sentimental,
simple as that, and I wrote you a letter about it. I lather up my
hands and rinse them under the warm water. I wish I'd appre-
ciated that moment more at the time. I should have asked you
about the different flowers, or at least paid more attention. Harebell, clover, ox-eye daisies and bird's-foot trefoil. That's what I
wrote to you: that I wanted to hear you say the name of every
single blade of grass and plant that's ever grown. That enough is
enough, that I'm done.

I know it was stupid, but I thought a letter might help you
remember for a while. That my handwriting might wake something inside you.

But now, in the cold light of day, I can see that was nonsense.

'What's the point?' I ask, fixing my eyes on myself.

I would skip today if I could. Just want to lock the door and curl
up under the blanket with Sixten. Don't want to talk to anyone.

But I hear the door in the kitchen again, and I rub my mouth
and hang the towel back on its little hook by the mirror with a sigh.

'Hi, Bo,' Johanna shouts, and some small part of me is glad that
she's the one who is here.


I wonder whether Johanna really thinks I need to take a shower.

'You have to wash regularly,' she says, draping her sweater over
the back of one of the kitchen chairs. 'Otherwise you'll smell like
a stinky old man.'

Her laugh is infectious. It makes her entire body shake, shoulders bobbing up and down. I turn to Sixten, who meets my eye.
What difference does it make if I stink? When Ture and I were up
at his cabin, we went weeks without washing, and I can't remember either of us smelling too bad even though I'm sure we must
have been filthy.

I shrug and stroke Sixten's head.

'I just don't feel like it today,' I say, struck by how serious I sound.

Sitting on the kitchen chair, she keeps looking at me, but she doesn't say anything. Then, without warning, her face breaks into a smile.

'That's fine. You can be a stinky old man if you want,' she says, getting up from the table.

She makes her way over to the fridge and takes out a bar of chocolate.

'But stinky old men need sweet treats, right?' She snaps the bar into smaller pieces and sets it on the table. 'Coffee?'

I lean back on the daybed. Stretch out my legs and smile at Johanna. Sixten jumps up beside me.

She brings a coffee over and then picks up my glasses to polish the lenses. Flicks through to the crossword in the local paper.

'Here,' she says, pushing it towards me. 'I started this while I was having breakfast. Let's see if you can finish it before me.'

She winks.

'I've heard stinky old men are pretty good at crosswords.'

*12.30 p.m.*

*Dumplings with meat sauce for lunch. Bo has a good appetite and cleans his plate. He says he tried to post a letter to Fredrika last night and that the patrol brought him home. We discuss taking a shower, but Bo isn't keen. Says a dip in the stream would be OK, but not a shower. Will try again later. Sixten seems happy and alert, took him out to pee.*

*Johanna*

THE MINUTE I close my eyes, I hear the screech of the sawblade. I reach up to adjust the pad on my right shoulder with aching arms. The leather strap is cutting into my left armpit. Up ahead, they're busy loading Arvid with more boards, which gives me a moment to catch my breath. To wipe the sweat from my brow. He, another stacker, and I collect the timber when it comes out of the saw as fresh boards. It's heavy work – they drive the logs in direct from the lake – and I'm always dropping my glove. It's so big it keeps slipping off, but there isn't much I can do other than bend down and pick it up again.

'Come on, Bo!'

I nod to Arvid before moving behind him and letting them load me up with five new boards as I gaze over towards the lake. Much prefer working down there. Catching the logs and carrying them up to the mill. Being so close to the water, being able to look across to the mountains in the distance.

The headache I woke with this morning has got worse, and the last board feels as heavy as two. At breakfast, I saw a notice that they're looking for men over in Hissmofors, and I wonder whether they have to work such long days there. Arvid is over by the stack, waiting for them to lift the last board from his shoulder, and I wish I were him. Still, just one more day to go, and then it'll be Sunday.

'Quit daydreaming! Next!' someone shouts.

I flinch and start walking towards the stack, where the wood is left to dry before being driven to the dealer in town. It's carefully stacked with narrow stickers in between, so the air can get through. I'm thirsty, and my head is pounding, I should take a break for a drink soon. The boards swing back slightly, and I adjust my hands to get a better grip.

Right then, my hand starts to slip out of the glove. I try to push it back in, upwards, but it's too late.

It all happens so quickly that I don't have time to think. I do everything I can to hold on to the boards, but my hand keeps slipping, and they fall to the left and hit Arvid. He doesn't notice a thing until they slam into his back, making him stumble forward over a loading pallet. The wood hits the ground, and so do I.

I'm back on my feet again in an instant.

'Shit!' I shout.

Arvid landed badly, with the boards on top of him. I see him sit up with a hand on his back, and I run over to him and crouch down. I feel so terrible, I wish the earth would swallow me up.

'Oof,' he says, but I can tell he's in pain.

It's one thing for me to be clumsy, but something else entirely if Arvid gets hurt as a result. As the thought crosses my mind, I realize that the frame saw has stopped and that everyone is staring at us.

'God, I slipped . . . the glove . . .' I manage to stammer, before someone drags me to my feet.

'Useless fucking oaf, you know to hold the pad properly.'

My old man's voice is shriller than the sawblade.

His hand strikes my cheek without warning, as unexpected as the fall a moment ago. I have to take a step back and shake my head, which usually helps the stinging to fade a bit quicker.

After a moment or two, I realize that a ring has formed around us. Someone has helped Arvid to his feet, and they walk him over to one of the lunch benches. I want to run after him, to apologize and make sure he's OK, but it's as if I'm frozen to the spot. Struggling to process what just happened. It's been a long time since my old man last hit me, and he's never done it in front of other people before.

'How fucking clumsy can you be?' he snarls, his eyes dark.

Two of the older men start stacking the boards I dropped.

'Second time this year. When're you going to learn?'

I don't speak, just stand with my eyes on the ground for what feels like an eternity. I feel the anger rising, but I can't manage a single word. What I want to do is scream that no one should treat their son the way he treats me, but I can't move a muscle.

I can feel the others' eyes on me, but no one speaks. Everyone is quiet. All I can hear is his voice, ringing in my ears.

In the end, the saw starts screeching again. I spot Jonasson, who is leaning against the post by the saw with a smirk on his face. The man is built like a brick shithouse, can lift an entire log with ease. He raises his right arm and tenses it, squeezing the muscle, and sneers at me. I pretend not to have noticed, just turn away and put my cap back on. I rub the back of my neck, then make my way over to the boards. Pull on my gloves while I watch my father, who is standing by the saw, guiding the logs in. There's no way I'll ever be able to do it that well, I think, as I try to swallow the lump in my throat. Maybe it's all in my head, but it feels as if everyone is staring at me. They probably think I'm as worthless as he does. That I've proved I'll never be able to handle the saw the way he can.

Once my shift is over, I sneak down to the edge of the lake to take a different route home. Don't want to go with my old man. Don't want to see him at all. Just want to get away.

I walk along the shore for a while before crossing the road and heading up to the woods by the last of the houses in Ranbyn. Past the avenue of birches on one of the farms, small buds on their slender branches. My stomach is growling, but I slow down as much as I can. I don't want to go home. Don't want to sit down to yet another evening at the same table as him.

I take the path to the little bridge over Renäsbäcken. Thanks to the melting snow in the mountains, the water in the stream is still high. When I reach the wooded meadow, I stop and crouch down beside an aspen. My body feels weary, and I sink to the ground and lean my head against the trunk, letting my thoughts drift back to what happened to Arvid. I spoke to him before we left, and he seemed OK. Wasn't angry or anything like that, but I still feel uneasy about the whole thing. Remember my father's reaction. Jonasson's. Really, though, it was the silence that hit me hardest, the way everyone just stood around as my father went on at me. I pull up a fistful of grass. I'm sixteen, for God's sake. Not a little boy he can push around. I pick a coltsfoot and hold it to my nose. It smells so strongly of spring, and the scent helps perk me up. I pick another couple, a little bouquet, and my mind drifts back to the ad I saw in the paper that morning. About the sawmill in Hissmofors that is looking for men. Surely I could get a job there.

'What the hell . . .' I mumble with a frown. 'I'll damn well . . .' I say, a little louder this time, getting to my feet and looking up at the crown of the tree. 'I'll damn well apply to Hissmofors!' I shout at the leaves, throwing the flowers to the ground.

The rush of energy that surges through me makes me forget just how hungry and tired I am, and I stand tall and start walking along the edge of the meadow.

Accommodation provided, the ad said. Bed, board, a place of my own. The thought gives me butterflies, and I feel like going straight home and packing a bag. I wonder if the bus goes all the way to Hissmofors or whether I'll have to walk from Krokom.

A sudden trumpeting sound interrupts those thoughts, and I see two majestic birds flying low overhead. The first cranes of the year. I pause to watch them. Their powerful wings, rhythmically beating the air and carrying their large bodies forward. Before they fly south again, I promise myself, I'll have left this place.

*5.15 p.m.*

*Fish balls. Sat down for a chat. Bo tells me about how they used to stack boards at the sawmill, about the shoulder pads they wore. That it took a while, but he really got the knack of it. Showers without a fuss!*

*Johanna*

# Tuesday
# 20 June

*8.15 a.m.*

*Bo asleep today, rain in the air . . . Mucus and coughing before porridge and a herring sandwich. Hans here. Given his meds.*

*Kalle*

HANS WAS here when I woke. He'd cancelled a meeting at work to come over. They called him yesterday afternoon to say that I'd been out and about during the night. As though I'd gone for a walk without any idea where I was going.

The microwave pings, and he takes out the porridge.

'Do you want lingonberry jam?' he asks, turning around.

I nod and brace myself against the daybed to sit up.

He sets the bowl down in front of me and adds a little milk. Puts the kettle on and takes out his phone, his thumb darting around the screen as the water boils.

'Ingrid and Olof, your caseworker, are coming over at ten,' he says without looking up. 'I thought I might take a work meeting from here. I'll go through to the living room.'

I nod and try the porridge. It's a little firm.

He fills a cup with water and adds a teabag.

'Sugar, right?'

'Yup.'

Sixten gets up from the floor and moves over to Hans, who gives him a pat on the head. He seems to be about to say something, but then closes his mouth. Puts the cup on the table, his eyes lingering on me.

'Thanks,' I say.

He hasn't mentioned what happened the night before last, other than to repeatedly say that this couldn't go on – at which I glared at him and wondered what couldn't.

'I'll get started on that meeting, then,' he says, giving me a look that suggests he is waiting for me to say something, I just don't know what.

'Righto.'

'It's online, so I'll be on my computer.'

'OK.'

'You can still use the toilet if you need to. I'll have headphones on, so you won't be interrupting.'

'OK.'

'See you in a little while, then,' he says, closing the living room door behind him.

I nod and lift a spoonful of porridge to my mouth. It's good to see the living room being used again. You were always the one who spent most time in there. It was where you kept your sewing machine, your wool, that sort of thing. But since you moved away, it's become little more than a corridor to the bathroom.

Sixten waits until I've finished eating to hop up beside me and lie down. He's like Buster in that sense: he likes to be close. And just like Buster, he knows that his food is whatever's in his bowl. No begging from either of them.

I turn on the radio and stretch out on the daybed. A woman with a low voice is talking, quick as anything. She barely even seems to pause for breath, and I struggle to keep up.

'That's true, of course,' a man interrupts, taking a deep breath. 'But men are already taking basically all their allocated time off.' He speaks much slower than her. 'And I see that as a strong argument in favour of individualizing parental leave.'

They seem to think that blokes should stay home with their kids as much as mothers do.

'Women are being left behind in their careers. They get stuck outside the labour market for several years, which means that financially speaking they're also worse off than men,' the woman with the fast voice continues.

I squeeze Sixten's ear. Hans and Sonja did the whole alternating parental leave thing. We could never understand why it had to be so complicated, almost as if you needed a degree just to understand how the system worked.

'It's my turn after Christmas,' Hans said during one Sunday lunch, when Ellinor was seven months old.

I was just about to say that Sonja having birthed the lass had to count for something, but you flashed me a look that silenced me. You smiled at Hans, but you didn't say anything either.

'These young people, they do what they want,' you said later, once he and the others had gone home.

What they want. Everyone does what they want nowadays. Things are the way they are for a reason. I remember looking at you as you measured out the coffee.

'Blokes aren't cut out for looking after little kids,' I grunted, thinking of my old man. About how bloody disastrous it would have been if he'd taken care of me. Those first few years with my mother, before I started school, were the best of my life. Just the two of us and the animals during the day. She taught me everything there was to know about life, and the less time he was at home, the better.

'You're probably right,' you said, moving the coffee pot to the stove. 'You're probably right.'

I close my eyes. I'm glad I don't have to worry about all that stuff. Don't know how they do it.

'A decent bloke looks after his wife so she can look after the kids, simple as that,' I mumble to Sixten, letting my eyelids droop.


'It needs sharpening first,' I say, holding the scythe up to my old man when he comes out.

He closes the door behind him without a word. We both know

that I'm much better with the grindstone than he is, and he shrugs and starts making his way towards the pigsty.

'What needs sharpening?'

I turn my head and realize that I'm lying on the daybed. Hans is coming towards me from the living room. I rub both eyes, and the sight of my old man's broad back fades.

'The scythe,' I say, raising my empty hand.

'There are no scythes here,' Hans replies, pausing in the middle of the room. 'You were dreaming.'

There is something tense about his mouth, and my hand drops back down to the blanket.

Hans opens the fridge and pours a glass of milk. He hands it to me, and I take a sip.

'We should re-do your bathroom, Dad.'

I look up at our son, and he can probably tell that I'm wondering why on earth we'd do something like that.

'It hasn't been touched in decades,' he says, as though there's something wrong with that.

'Touched?'

'Yeah, it's been the same for the past forty years. The shower is constantly dripping, for example.'

Hans pulls out a chair and sits down opposite me. He has that look on his face, the one that tells me he knows best. Because he's been to university and travelled all over the world.

'That's because they don't turn the tap far enough,' I say.

'No, it's because everything's old and needs replacing,' he counters, going through the post he'd brought in with him. 'Don't you think it would be nice to have some underfloor heating, too?'

Has he lost his mind? Does he seriously think I should have a new bathroom fitted – and one with underfloor heating, at that?

'It'd help your joints,' he adds. 'The doctor says heat is good.'

Our son is sitting with the electricity bill in his hands. Doesn't he realize that I'm going to die soon? I would barely have time to use up the water in the tank before it was curtains for me.

I'm tired, and I close my eyes. Imagine Hans walking around the house on his own. Emptying the freezer of all the ready meals he bought. Putting them into a couple of paper bags and taking them home.

No, he would probably just toss them in the bin.

*11.10 a.m.*

*Ingrid, Hans and Olof here. Meeting about introduction of night patrol, plus the Sixten situation. We agree that the night patrol will check on Bo from tomorrow and that Sixten will stay here for the time being, that the carers will take him for walks when they can. Ingrid takes primary responsibility.*

*Ingrid*

I STARE up at the ceiling and prick my ears. They've forgotten that the kitchen window is open. Ingrid will tell me about the meeting later, I'm sure, but I still want to hear everything they're saying out there.

'Walking people's dogs isn't your job, Ingrid,' says Hans. 'I know Sixten means a lot to him, but this can't go on.'

They're quiet for a moment, and I feel the anger rising. He's so narrow-minded, our son. Who the hell cares about whose responsibility it is when it comes to a dog, I feel like shouting through the window.

'It's part of the job to me,' Ingrid replies, in that calm way only she can, so firmly that it makes me loosen my grip on Sixten's collar slightly.

'But it's not just that,' Hans continues. 'He keeps going out into the woods with him. He could trip, break a leg, get stuck there.'

I can't see him, but I can imagine his body language. Reaching up to tug on his right earlobe, almost like he's massaging himself.

I don't know how I feel, because I keep changing my mind. He sounds so miserable that I want to get up and open the door, tell him that it's OK and that everything will be fine. But at the same time, I can't understand why he is arguing with Ingrid, why he thinks Sixten should live somewhere else. It's as if he really does want to hurt me.

'I know you're worried about Bo,' says Ingrid. I hold my breath. 'But we've agreed that Sixten will stay here for the time being, and I'll take care of him. It's as simple as that.'

My eyes start to well up, and though Sixten and I are alone in the room, I close them.

They stop talking again, and the ticking of the clock takes over. I wonder if they've just lowered their voices, but then I hear Olof.

'OK, then we're agreed.' He has barely said a word since he arrived, the caseworker from town with an office in Frösön. He has to be here whenever any new decisions are made, but he never seems to have much input himself. 'We introduce night patrol and leave Sixten here for now.'

Relief washes over me, but I also know that Hans won't give up that easily. I can't afford to pin all my hopes on Ingrid, not in the long run. I'll have to come up with some other way of making him see sense. Of getting him to understand just how wrong it would be to take Sixten.

Ellinor, of course! I get up and shuffle over to the calendar, squint at it. Sure enough: she's coming to visit in eleven days.

Back on the daybed, I take a piece of paper from the pad on the table and scrawl *Ring Ellinor*. The minute Hans has gone, I'll try to get in touch with her. As I lower the pen, I have the feeling that there was something about Ellinor that I wanted to tell Hans, but I can't remember what it was.

INGRID IS in the kitchen, doing the washing up after Hans and Olof have gone. They came in together, drank coffee, ate some almond tarts and presented their 'suggestions', as they put it. As though I could disagree.

Ingrid tells me that we'll take things one day at a time, and I believe her. She turns off the tap and dries her hands on the towel, then hangs it back on its hook by the counter. You always used to drape it over the handle on the oven door.

She pulls out a chair and sits down opposite me.

'What did you write in your letter, then?'

'What?'

'You said you went out to post a letter to Fredrika the other night. What did you write?'

'Oh,' I say, though I feel the weight on my chest lift.

Ingrid's eyes are still on me.

'It was a dream,' I say. 'Or a memory, really. I guess you could say I dreamed about a memory.'

I cough and spit into my cup. Ingrid hands me a piece of kitchen roll.

'What sort of memory?'

'It's a bit silly,' I say.

She nods for me to go on.

'It was the Midsummer before we got married, Fredrika and me. She dragged me out to pick flowers in the middle of the night. You know the old tradition: if you put seven different kinds under your pillow, you'll dream about your future spouse. She wanted to make sure I was the one.'

I trail off, my cheeks hot.

'Sounds like a smart move on her part,' says Ingrid. 'Guess she didn't want to buy a pig in a poke.'

I laugh.

'No, guess not.'

'You got married though, so she must have dreamed about you that night?'

'So she said,' I reply, unable to hold back the laughter.

You came running towards me the very next day.

'You were with me all night. That's so strange, isn't it?' you said, and I don't know which of us laughed harder. I picked you up and twirled you around and around.

The phlegm catches in my throat, and I spit into the cup again, as hard as I can. Ingrid gets up to fetch a glass of water. She moves so easily, barely a sound as she crosses the room.

'Here,' she says, holding the glass out to me.

I take a sip, and my throat immediately feels a little clearer.

'I don't think either of us really believes in the whole Midsummer flowers thing,' she says after a moment, taking a seat again. 'But you were pretty bloody lucky that it wasn't some other bloke who showed up in her dreams that night.'

TURE STRIDES across the room. He grips the edge of the bed, swings his right leg up and heaves himself on to the top bunk. Straightens his long legs and folds his arms beneath the pillow with a deep sigh.

I close the door on the stove and let my eyes scan the room as I stretch my back. The log walls are dark from the countless fires that have been lit here over the years, subduing the September light that filters in through the two small windows. A stubborn fly thuds against one of the panes, and I roll up an old newspaper and take aim. It drops to the sill after my very first attempt, and I open the window and nudge it outside.

I go out on to the porch to get the bag of char Ture put into a bucket of water to keep them cool. Make my way down to the stream and lower the bucket into the deepest spot, then crouch down and gut and rinse the fish in the cold, rippling water. A few metres away, the leaves on the tiny, gnarled birches have started to turn yellow. The cabin is right at the treeline, and it's so quiet that the noise from the stream is almost deafening.

When I get back inside, Ture is sitting on a chair with a bucket of spuds between his feet.

'Perfect, I could do with a bit of water,' he says, leaning back.

I kick off my boots and carry it over.

'I'm not used to being retired yet,' I say, pouring some of the water into the bucket in front of him. 'My body feels like it still has to go back to work.'

Ture picks up a potato and brushes a lump of soil from the skin. As ever, you sent us up here with several kilos of them.

'It'll come,' he says, reaching for another. 'It'll come. Must've taken me at least a year. Kept going away at the weekend when I could just as easily have gone on a Tuesday.'

I nod and place the fish on the counter. Have never been one for travelling, but I know what he means.

I take the salt down from the shelf. I've been coming here for so long that, in some ways, the cabin feels like my own – though of course I don't have childhood memories of the place the way Ture does.

'Have you come up here every year?' I ask, giving the fish a good salt. Don't be stingy, you always say when I ask how much to toss in.

He turns his head towards the window.

'There were a few years after I hit twenty when I didn't come, but other than that, pretty much,' he says dropping a spud into the pan. 'Is five enough for you?'

I nod. Add a healthy knob of butter to the cast-iron pan and set it on the stove.

'Needed a break from Hissmofors, you know? Needed to see somewhere else.'

I can understand why he wanted to get away; you told me about all the gossip. It's not something you ever brought up any more. After a while, I think you just accepted our friendship, and we don't really talk about Ture. There's nothing left to say.

'So you went to Gothenburg,' I fill in.

'Mmm, I went to Gothenburg.'

He has told me about the city on the west coast. The ships, the cranes, the fish markets. The trams. Sometimes I wonder what it would be like to visit him there, because he still goes down to Gothenburg quite often. I could pack a bag, get on the train and have him meet me at the station, but so far it hasn't happened.

I stick a fork into the lump of butter, which has started to melt.

Move it around the pan and remember when I first moved to Hissmofors.

'It felt so bloody good to get away from my old man,' I say. 'When I left Renäs. Not having him there all the time, sticking his nose into everything. Things always had to be done his way, and there was no bloody arguing with him. You know how it was: he'd kick up a hell of a stink if I even stacked the wood in a different place.'

Ture gives me a quick look of understanding and moves the pot over to the stove. He's quieter than usual. Then again, he often gets like this out here. As though he slows down.

'They're just too set in their ways, that generation,' he says after a moment.

The pan sizzles when I add the fish. I move it towards the edge of the stove, and it settles down. Ture doesn't seem to have noticed. His eyes are fixed on something outside.

He hasn't told me much about his parents. All I know is that his father died young and his mother was in a home.

'Was he like that too? Your old man?' I ask after a pause.

Ture lets out a long sigh and shrugs.

'Yeah, he was a difficult bastard,' he says, getting to his feet.

He grabs a couple of plates and some cutlery from the top drawer and sets the table.

I nod. They probably all were.

'Wasn't too keen on my Storsjö Beast collection, let me tell you,' he says with a devilish twinkle in his eye.

'I bet.'

I glance over at Ture, who is standing by the handmade counter. It must have been tough. I don't doubt for a second that my old man would've thrown me out if I'd been like him.

'It's kind of nice they've all croaked,' he says turning around. His face grows serious. 'I'm probably not supposed to say that, am I?'

I shrug, and neither of us speaks. We wait for the fish to finish cooking.

I've never thought of it that way before, but he's right. I push the spatula under the fish to stop them from sticking. It was good when my father died, but it also feels wrong to think like that. Ture is brave for saying that sort of thing. For just coming out with it, what he really thinks. And it's reassuring that we seem to feel the same way.

He takes out two pot rests and puts them on the table, and I set the heavy iron pan down with a thud.

'Glad to see you kept the heads on,' he says, looking down at the fish. 'Makes them much more tender.'

I nod and dig two pieces of flatbread out of the bag you gave us, tear them into decent chunks. Ture adds a dollop of mash to each bit of bread and then sits down. We start by nibbling on the crispy skins.

'A lemming ran by while I was getting the water,' I say, as thrilled to tell him about it as I was when I spotted it. There must be a lot of them about this year, because we saw at least a dozen dead lemmings on the way up here.

Ture grins and debones the fish.

'Hey, good for you,' he says, adding a little flesh on top of the mashed potato and rolling up his bread. 'You were so worried about the little buggers on the drive up.'

'Pff,' I say, though I can't help but laugh.

The aroma of fried fish fades, and the ticking of the clock on the wall takes over. I rub some life into my eyes and see Johanna doing something over by the counter. Sixten presses up against my left leg. My very own bedwarmer. I stroke his neck and yawn.

*6.25 p.m.*

*Bo fast asleep when I arrive. Wanted mash and char for dinner, had to make do with fish balls in sauce. Took Sixten for a quick walk.*

*Johanna*

# Saturday
# 1 July

*8.15 a.m.*

*Porridge and medication. Bo in a good mood, wanted to shower. Saw on the calendar that Ellinor is coming this afternoon.*

*Johanna*

I DON'T need to check the calendar to remember that Ellinor is coming today. It's the first thing that crosses my mind when I wake. Ellinor, our bumblebee, has always looked after her old grandad.

I yawn and rub my face.

'Here you go,' says Johanna, placing a bowl of porridge in front of me.

I force myself up as she adds milk, making it runny.

It's still early, but it feels warm. Johanna is wearing a green T-shirt and jeans. She's only a few years older than Ellinor, and I went to school with her grandad. He was one of those people who never said much, kept himself to himself. A few of the boys used to play marbles after school, and he would sometimes tag along. The rest of us would critique each other's throws, but he often seemed lost in thought. Hell of a carver he was, though. His missus sold the things he made at the Christmas market every year.

'Nice hooks,' Johanna said with a smile, the first time she came over here and hung her coat up by the door. She must have seen them in plenty of other people's houses, too, because those coat hooks of his were popular.

My fingers are always stiffest in the morning, and I struggle to lift my spoon. In the end, I push it halfway off the edge of the table so I can grip the handle.

'Has he been out?' Johanna asks, turning to Sixten, who is lying on the floor.

I try to remember. There are days when I wake up around four and take him out to do his business, but I'm not sure whether I did that this morning.

'No, I don't think so,' I say hesitantly. Don't want to make it seem like I don't know what's what.

Johanna digs her phone out of her back pocket and checks the time.

'You eat your porridge, and I'll take him out for a quick wee before your shower.'

Today isn't technically a shower day, but Johanna thinks we can make an exception because Ellinor is coming. I don't argue; I just nod. Don't want to be a stinky old man when Ellinor gets here.

I manage to finish my porridge before Johanna comes back, and I decide to clear the table, but she opens the door before I have time to do anything other than stack the newspapers. Sixteen trots over to say hello, then leaps up on to the daybed. Spots an opportunity to curl up at the very end, with his head on my pillow.

'Are you ready, then?' I ask, holding my arms out as Johanna comes into the kitchen.

She laughs. 'Honestly, Ellinor should come to see you every week. Just think how clean you'd be.'

'Pah,' I say, though I can't help smiling. 'Come on.'

I turn around and start making my way through to the bathroom. Johanna is right behind me, ready to catch me if I fall. I'm pretty slow, but she doesn't seem too bothered.

Ture tends to get undressed and sit naked on the toilet lid to wait for his carers, so he's ready when they arrive. The problem with that is they're not always on time, which means he has to sit there waiting for an eternity.

'I get stressed when they're stressed,' he explained, when I told him that surely wasn't necessary.

Personally, I don't care whether they're stressed or not; I take my time. I do think it's a hell of a lot of showering for one person, though. I've never showered as much as I have over the past few years, and that's even with me refusing every now and again. What difference does it make if I stink when there's no one here to smell me?

'There you go,' says Johanna, spreading a towel on the toilet lid so that it isn't so cold for me to sit on.

She stretches above me to reach the corner cupboard where they keep all their plastic aprons and gloves.

'Let's see, then,' she says, double-checking her apron is straight. 'Shall we start with your shirt?'

'Sounds good,' I say, lifting my chin so that she can undo the top button.

Sixten appears in the doorway. He pricks up his ears and stares in, seems to think this is all a load of fuss.

'Maybe we should get him into the shower too, while we're at it?' Johanna suggests, opening her eyes wide and sticking her tongue out.

I laugh.

'That'd be something, huh?'

Before long, I'm stark naked on the toilet, waiting for her to start the shower. The bathroom is warm. Hans must have turned on the radiator without mentioning it, because he knows I think it's unnecessary.

'Is the temperature OK?' she asks, holding the showerhead out to me.

I hold my arm beneath the water and tell her it's fine. She rinses the shower seat, and I make my way into the shower and sit down.

'Here it comes, then,' she says, before she directs the jets at my stiff feet. My toes are so crooked – just like my mother's – that it's hard to believe they're actually toes. 'Temperature still OK?'

I nod, and she works her way upwards. I feel a tingle as the water runs down my back, and I close my eyes for a moment.

'Here,' she says, handing me the showerhead.

She squeezes a big blob of shower gel into her hand and lathers me up. Pushes a finger between each toe. It tickles, but it also feels good.

'Why don't we do this more often?' I ask.

Johanna grins and meets my eye.

'Oh, Bo. You say the same thing every time.'

1.30 p.m.

*Bo meets me out in the garden and wants to test-drive my
car. Nice and comfy, says he's keen to do a deal ASAP. In
a good mood, looking forward to seeing Ellinor. Showered
and smelling good! Potato gratin and turkey for lunch.
Took Sixten for a quick walk.*

*Kalle*

THE SHOWER must have taken a lot of energy, because I'm hungry even though Kalle just gave me lunch. I get up to make myself a sandwich.

My eyes come to rest on the note Hans put up to remind me to eat. The moisture and fumes from cooking have left the paper crinkled, and one corner has started to curl inwards.

The fridge is full of things I like, and the sight of the beers, jellied veal, rice pudding and fermented milk makes me feel warm inside. The same brands and products you and I used to buy. We didn't do too badly with him after all, our son.

The front door opens, and I feel a sudden rush. Know Ellinor must be here. I take a bar of chocolate out of the fridge and put it on the table.

The house immediately feels cosier the moment I see her. She holds out her arms and practically leaps into the kitchen.

'Grandad!'

Her hug almost makes me lose my balance, but I chuckle and stroke her fair hair, which is even longer than last time.

'I'm growing it so it'll cover my boobs,' she says, as I lightly take a lock between my fingers.

She has always been like this: not embarrassed to say anything. The polar opposite of her dad, who clams up at the drop of a hat. Ellinor is like Ture in that sense; the conversation has always flowed. I've never had to think all that much when I'm with her. Never had to tiptoe around her like I have with Hans.

I wonder how our granddaughter could have turned out so different from her father. Maybe that's down to Sonja, to something she did with Ellinor that we didn't do with Hans.

Sixten trots over and presses his head to the side of her thigh, nudging her hand with his snout. She laughs and crouches down in front of him.

'Hello, you old goat. How are you doing?' she asks, stroking his head.

'Oh, there's nothing wrong with him,' I say, standing tall.

Ellinor reaches for one of his toys, and Sixten immediately grabs it. I've always loved seeing her play with him, and I spot my opening.

'But they still want to take him away. I'm guessing you've heard?'

She throws Sixten's toy across the room, watching as he darts after it.

'Your dad's lost the plot, if you ask me.'

Sixten runs back with the toy in his mouth, wanting her to throw it again, but she just puts it down on the floor in front of her and scratches him behind the ear.

'He says I can't take care of him, that he isn't getting enough exercise, but since when has Hans cared about animals?' I ask, coming down with a coughing fit when I attempt to laugh.

Ellinor passes me the spit jar, and I turn around and clear my throat. She pulls out a chair and sits down. Sixten follows her, lowering his head on to her lap.

The coughing has left me so drained that I have to lie down.

'Either way, you need to talk some sense into him,' I say, my head heavy on the pillow. A feeling of calm spreads through me.

Ellinor is sitting quietly, still not looking at me. Has something happened? It's not like her to be this quiet.

'Yeah, Dad mentioned that there'd been a bit of fuss over Sixten,' she says after a moment.

So, the bastard has already managed to put his mad ideas into her head. I try to clench my fist, but my fingers won't bend. Clearly everyone but me gets to have a say in what happens in my life.

Our granddaughter picks at the sleeve of her top.

Then she looks up. I meet her eye, and I see the same thing I saw in Hans's recently. Something that tells me the roles have been reversed. Something compassionate but superior.

'Dad is right, actually,' she says, which sends an ache through my chest. 'It's hard for you to take him out.'

I can't believe what I'm hearing. Never thought I'd see the day.

'Please don't be mad,' she sighs, letting her arms drop to her sides. 'Sixten needs longer walks.'

As though I don't know what a hound needs.

I close my eyes, don't want to see her. My head is spinning, and I feel sick.

After everything I've done for you, I want to scream. After all the toys and treehouses I built, all the times I drove you to football practice. She tells me that she knows it isn't easy, and I want to scream that a twenty-one-year-old doesn't know a bloody thing, but something stops me. I don't want to scream, not at Ellinor. Instead, I scrunch up my eyes and keep my mouth shut.

'Please, Grandad, look at me.'

I reluctantly open my eyes. She seems so upset that I actually stop feeling angry for a moment. I don't want to hurt her.

'I just think Sixten would be happier with a family,' she says, putting a hand on my leg. I think I can feel it trembling.

The situation is so absurd that I can't manage a single word. The last of my energy deserts me, and I lie in silence as our bumblebee betrays me. I don't know why, but it feels much worse for Ellinor to let me down than Hans. I didn't see it coming.

I fix my eyes on a knot on the wooden ceiling, and all I know right now is that I don't want any of this. I don't want to go on.

# Wednesday
## 12 July

*8.15 a.m.*

*Medicine given + blown into bottle. Bo stubborn, won't eat his porridge. Wants me to take dog out. No time.*

*Eva-Lena*

THE MINUTE the door closes, I reach for the jar with your scarf. I try as hard as I can, but I can't get the lid off. Instead, I let it slide down beside me, put a hand on Sixten's head and close my eyes. Let the kitchen fade away.

I jump off the bike and wheel it across the road. Sitting on the pannier rack, Hans is gripping our rods tightly. The fish we caught is in the rucksack. It's such a calm, quiet evening that we can hear even the slightest breath of wind. The lingering summer light made us lose track of ourselves while we were down at the lake, and I have no idea what time it is now, but you'll probably think we're a little late. Hans's eyes lock on to the pigs as we pass the Larssons' place, their huge bodies lumbering around in the muck. They must be at least ten times his size.

I squint up the hill, trying to work out whether I have the energy to keep cycling, but I decide to push the bike instead. It won't do the lad any harm to get to bed a bit later than usual. My eyes drift across the meadow, towards the edge of the wood, and I spot three cranes, two big and one small. I pause and give Hans a gentle nudge to get his attention.

'Wha—'

'Shhh,' I tell him, holding a finger to my lips and nodding towards the family of birds.

His eyes widen.

'The baby has probably just learned to fly,' I whisper into his ear.

They have taken cover by the treeline, and their magnificent tail feathers shake as they wander around, pecking at the ground.

'And now they're going to fatten themselves up,' I continue. 'Before they head south for the autumn.'

Hans nods thoughtfully.

We're standing so close, but they don't seem bothered by us. I guess we must blend in with the summer night. There is something special about being able to watch wild animals like this. A glimpse into the way life works, somehow.

Then something hits the gravel track, and the family of cranes flap away. The tin of worms is lying on its side by the back wheel.

I give Hans an irritated glance as he tries to adjust the fishing rods in his arms, and I'm just about to open my mouth and snap at him, tell him he's an oaf, when he looks up at me.

'Sorry,' he mumbles.

The look on his face is so sad. I used to feel the same shakiness I think I can see in him whenever my old man looked at me, and I close my mouth and try to swallow the lump in my throat.

'It . . .' I begin, putting a hand on his slim back. 'It doesn't matter.'

He looks down.

'I'm tired,' he says after a moment, yawning.

The can of worms rolls slowly towards my foot, and I bend down and pick it up, pass it to him.

'We'd better head home then, eh?' I say, climbing back on to the bike.

As we pass the Larssons' mailbox, the cranes reappear above the trees, flying right overhead. I imagine I can feel the downbeat from their wings, and there is nowhere else I'd rather be.

'Dad.'

When I turn to look at Hans, he is sitting quietly, his eyes on the mountains.

'Dad.' There it is again. 'Dad. Hello?'

His voice is coming from the porch, dragging me out of my dream.

'You need to get rid of this, Dad.'

I open my eyes and see our son irritably holding up one of your jackets. He looks stressed.

'You can't just have her stuff lying all over the place, as though she still lives here,' he continues.

When I close my eyes and press my fist between Sixten's head and the daybed, I hear him sigh. I try to cling on to sleep, but it's gone.

Who the hell does he think he is? Coming over here and telling me what to do with your things. What difference does it make if your jacket is still hanging in the hallway?

I feel the urge to get up, to thump the table and tell him I'll do whatever the hell I want. That I'm the captain of this ship.

But I don't, because I'm not the captain. I'm a useless lump who's been tied to the mast in a storm.

Hans folds the jacket and puts it in the carrier bag on the kitchen counter. I lie quietly, watching him. Remember that Mother kept my old man's things, left them right where they'd always been, and I never said a word about it. I pat Sixten and wonder why Hans can't just leave things be. Why he constantly has to stick his nose in and cause trouble.

Then he turns around, and I catch a glimpse of what I think might be compassion in his eyes.

I study our fifty-seven-year-old son. There's nothing that compares to that, to raising a child. No one ever said a word about it before you got pregnant. That it would be this hard. How can something as natural as starting a family be so complicated?

I rub Sixten's head and think about the deal I made with myself. That I need to fix things before my time is up. That I don't want there to be any hard feelings between us at the end. I don't want him to have to worry about a thing.

Hans takes your jacket into the porch and then comes back

into the kitchen with a paper bag of food. A sense of weariness hits me, as though I've spent an entire day walking and now have to do the same all over again.

'The jam you liked was on special offer,' he says, holding up the Coop bag.

The look on his face is so warm, and his crooked smile reminds me of you. For a moment or two, it feels like you're right here with us.

*1.15 p.m.*

*Hans and Assistive Services here to set up the adapted bed. Sausage casserole for lunch.*

*Kalle*

THEY'VE PLONKED me in a kitchen chair by the window, at a safe distance from what they're doing, so I can watch as they lug out the wooden daybed where Sixten and I have spent every single night since you moved to Brunkullagården. The daybed from your parents' house, which we brought from Hissmofors when we moved here.

I've been against them swapping it for what they call an 'adapted bed' ever since Hans first mentioned the idea. I sleep best on the daybed, but my wheezing words don't carry much weight any more. They drop like dead birds from the sky, landing in a place no one ever goes.

Hans's forehead is glistening, but the man from the flea market barely seems to have broken a sweat. He's much more muscular than our son, and probably at least twenty years younger. I wonder how much he'll sell it for.

Sixten is anxious, and though my hand is on his back he lets out a low whine.

That's when I notice the van outside.

'Did they really have to park there?'

'What?' Hans turns around.

'Do you know how much those paving stones cost?' It was a big investment when we decided to lay them.

'Not now, Dad.'

Hans lifts up one end of the daybed and nudges a towel beneath its legs so that they can pull it across the floor more easily.

I sense my irritation growing. I want to shout, but for some reason my feelings seem pathetic. As though no one on earth would think I have the right to be angry about this.

I make my way through to the bathroom so I can think in peace. The man from the flea market lowers the daybed so I can get past.

'OK, let's try again,' Hans says with a sigh.


By the time I get back, they've already loaded it into the van. Hans pushes the new bed into the corner of the kitchen and locks the wheels. At least I was allowed to decide where it went. In the same place the daybed has always been.

We stand in silence once the van has driven away, staring at the bed. The clock ticks loudly on the wall. It looks like a hospital bed, the kind you slept in on the maternity ward after Hans was born. The kind I slept in after my heart operation. That you sleep in every night now.

Seeing our son's look of satisfaction, I feel like grabbing a bit of firewood and hurling it at his head, but I don't have the energy. If he spent even half the time he puts into invading my home and stirring up trouble on walking Sixten, there wouldn't be a problem.

'Why do I need a bed with all these handles, rails and wheels?' I ask with a frown as I sit down, keen to do everything I can to be difficult.

'Because it's much better for you,' Hans replies, wiping the sweat from his brow. His body might be big and fat, but he's still so weak.

I spit into the cup I'm holding, see that it bothers him.

'How can it be better for me when it's not what I want?'

My voice breaks. I'm so damn tired of everyone else deciding what's best for me.

'This one is much easier to get up out of. Watch.' Hans lies down on the neatly made bed and pulls himself up using the grip handle that hangs from an aluminium pole at the end of the mattress.

I briefly consider getting up and beating him with the handle. Sixten lowers his head to my skinny thigh, and I feel reinvigorated. This is my bloody house. I steel myself and cough hard enough to dislodge the phlegm.

'How can this be better when I *know* I sleep like a log on the daybed?'

Hans sighs. 'But it's not just about you, Dad.'

How can that be true, I want to scream, when it's the place where *I* sleep that we're talking about, but my throat has filled again and I start coughing instead.

'Here,' Hans says after a moment, handing me a glass of water. 'You know these beds make it easier for the carers to help you.'

My newfound strength deserts me as quickly as it arrived, and I give up and let Hans get me into the bed so he can show me all the clever things the remote control can do. Nodding and humming as he raises the backrest.

Hans heads home, and I lean back in the bed, defeated. It's so soft that it feels like it might swallow me up. Sixten is in his basket on the floor, didn't want to hop up beside me when Hans patted the mattress.

'Come on, we don't have any choice,' I say, gently hitting my thigh.

He gives me a hesitant look then jumps up. Spins around a few times, and lies down by my left side as usual.

When I close my eyes, I see Hans walking down the trail to Ture's cabin ahead of me. His rucksack is full, and he is carrying his sleeping bag and camping mat himself.

'Don't make him carry too much,' you said, as I re-packed his bag and shoved another sweater in. 'He's only nine.'

'Only nine,' I parroted.

At his age, I was carrying much heavier loads. But I told you that was the last thing and smiled.

Ture has found himself a walking stick, and now Hans is looking for one too.

'There!'

'No, it's too thin,' says Ture. 'Keep looking.'

Winter is just around the corner; I can feel it in the air. The
temperature will probably dip below zero tonight. Hans has been
talking about this trip for weeks, which fishing rods we're going
to take and what we're going to do. He's been joining us since he
was six. You thought he was too young to walk so far before that.
I thought he was big enough to come a year earlier, but you put
your foot down.

Ture and Hans are walking in line further down the trail. The
first time he came to visit after we got home from hospital with
Hans, he toned down his usual chattiness. I hadn't told him that
you'd had a difficult birth, but he'd picked up on it. He smiled
warmly at you, as you sat in the armchair with a sleeping Hans in
your arms. Fetched you a jug of water and a glass.

'I hear it's thirsty work.'

You gave him a cautious nod in return.

Before long, Hans woke up and his little mouth opened in a
big yawn.

'Maybe you'd like to hold him, Ture?' you asked. I was surprised, but I didn't say a word, just watched from my chair at the
kitchen table.

'I'd love to,' said Ture, his eyes widening in that dramatic way
of his.

And so I sat there, watching my friend hold my newborn son.
It felt important somehow, that he got to be part of Hans's life.

Ture leaned in over his tiny body.

'Once you're a bit older, you can join us big boys when we go
fishing at the cabin,' he said in a silly voice.

You and I both laughed. There was something about his tone
and his tall, gangly frame paired with Hans's gurgling that seemed
so funny.

'There, Hans!' Ture says without warning. 'Over by the birch. That's your stick!'

Hans leaps through bilberry bushes and runs over to the birch Ture had pointed out.

'Perfect,' Ture tells him when he gets back. He breaks off the small side shoots and hands it back to Hans.

After dinner that evening, I stretch out on the bottom bunk. It's starting to get dark outside, but I never bother with any of the bedtime stuff you're so particular about at home. Let the lad stay up until we hit the hay. I can't remember ever having a bedtime when I was his age. I think we all just turned in after dinner.

'Which book did you bring?' Hans asks.

Ture moves over to his rucksack and triumphantly produces a fat tome. 'This one!'

I squint over at him in the soft glow of the paraffin lamp, but I can't make out the title. He puts it down on the table in front of Hans, who starts to sound the words out.

'Grrimms' Faairry Taaaalesss.'

Hans has taken his time learning to read, but he is really getting the hang of it now. Has always liked other people reading to him, too.

'Exactly. Very good,' says Ture, opening the book at a story about Cinderella.

'Isn't that one pretty horrible?' I ask. I remember you talking about it with one of your sisters; her kids had nightmares, apparently.

'It's got its moments,' Ture mumbles, pushing his glasses on to the bridge of his nose. 'But a bit of nastiness never hurt anyone. I loved these stories when I was a boy.'

Ture starts reading, and I want to listen, but he hasn't said more than a few sentences before I doze off. I catch the odd word every now and again, hear the fire crackling, then I drift away again.

'Dad, they're chopping bits of their feet off!' Hans shouts, tugging on my arm.

'What are you talking about?' I murmur, still drowsy.

At the table, Ture chuckles.

'The stepsisters are cutting parts of their feet off – a toe and a heel – so that the glass slipper will fit and they'll meet their prince,' he explains.

I rub my face.

'What a load of rubbish,' I say with a yawn. 'It's all made up, Hans.'

You wouldn't have thought it was a good idea for him to read that sort of thing.

'I want a different story tomorrow,' says Hans, turning to Ture. 'How about the one about Rapunzel?'

'Yeah, yeah,' I say, nodding, even though I have no idea who that is. I get up and make my way over to the door. 'I'm going out for a nice evening pee. Coming?'

Hans and I walk away from the cabin, to a small rise. Under the full moon, the lake and forest are bathed in cold light. Behind us, the Kalfjället Mountains are silent.

Hans stays close by as he tugs down his fly, his arm against the side of my leg. He doesn't say a word.

'You know it's all just make believe, don't you? Those stories Ture reads.'

He gives me an uncertain shrug and aims the stream of pee at the heather.

'The way he tells them almost makes them seem real, doesn't it?' I say, patting him on the shoulder.

We shake off the last few droplets and trudge back towards the cabin. Hans reaches up and takes my hand, gripping it tight. I squeeze his little hand back.

*5.45 p.m.*

*Made rice pudding, but Bo doesn't want any. Wants me to write that he's not happy with his new bed. Says it's too soft.*

*Ingrid*

I'm drenched in sweat when I wake, and there's a weight on my chest. The same sentence keeps going round and round in my head, cutting away at me like a sharp knife.

*If he can take your daybed then he can take Sixten.*

I pull myself up into a sitting position and reach for my phone with shaking fingers. Talking to Ture feels urgent right now. It takes me a while to find the phone, because the bed is higher than the daybed, and I'm still not quite used to it. I push the green button. Manage to hit *Hans* instead of *Ture*, and the call goes through.

'What the hell,' I mutter, pressing the red button as quickly as I can.

Sixten lifts his head, while the phone rings for what feels like for ever.

Ture eventually picks up. 'Bo, hello.'

Hearing his voice helps calm me down.

'Did we agree to talk today?' he asks, clearing his throat.

'No, no . . . but I wanted to call anyway,' I say, immediately trailing off.

'Has something happened?'

The question makes me feel like crying. I don't want any of this, I want to scream. I want him to ring Hans and say there's no way in hell you're going to take Sixten from Bo.

'Bo, are you there?'

'I'll kill myself if they take Sixten away,' I say, before I have time to think.

Ture clears his throat again.

'Those are strong words, Bo.'

I don't know what else to say, so I just stroke Sixten. Images of the Fredrikssons' boy flicker by. They found him in the barn with his head blown off on his twentieth birthday.

'Do you really think you would?' Ture asks after a moment.

'What?'

'You know, kill yourself, if they took Sixten,' he says with a grunt.

I think it over for a moment. If I were a hunter, it probably wouldn't be so difficult. But for someone like me, without any guns, who can't even manage to shower on his own and can barely use the toilet? There's no way.

'I don't know . . .' I say, letting the sentence ebb away.

He is quiet on the other end of the line.

'Eh,' I say. 'It is what it is.'

Ture grunts again, and I feel a slight pang of shame. I sigh and lower a hand to my knee. My fingers are aching more than usual.

'Eh,' I say again.

Ture still hasn't said a word, and I start to wonder whether he might have hung up on me, because it isn't like him to be so quiet. I'm just about to say that it was stupid of me, that I'd never do it, when he clears his throat.

'I don't want you to do that. I don't want that to happen,' he says, in a tone I don't recognize.

His hand must be shaking, because I hear the cup rattling as he lowers it on to the saucer.

I'm ashamed, remember the Fredrikssons, that they were never the same again. I wouldn't want to put Ture through anything like that.

'No, of course,' I say, trailing a finger over a coffee stain on my trouser leg. 'Of course I won't.'

'Besides, they haven't taken Sixten yet,' he says in his normal tone. 'I think Ingrid will sort things out, and maybe Hans will see sense after all.'

I can still feel the clawing sensation in my chest, but the weight does seem to have lifted a little.

# Tuesday
# 18 July

SIXTEN IS standing in the middle of the kitchen floor with his ears pricked and his eyes on me, the way he often does when he needs to pee. I lower the phone to the table. Marita just called to ask how everything was, whether I needed help, and I promised to let her know if anything came up. Briefly considered telling her about Sixten, then decided against it. She probably has enough on her plate as it is.

I'm tired, and what I really want is to stay right here in bed, but I grab the handle above my head and pull myself up.

I must have dozed off during breakfast, because the cup of tea in front of me is cold. The edges of the bread have hardened, too, but the whey butter is still soft. Sixten spins around on the floor and trots over to the door to wait for me to put on his collar.

I feel dizzy as I get up, and I have to grip the edge of the table until the dark spots disappear. Can't remember where I left my slippers. The hard floor hurts my feet without them.

Sixten darts out the minute I open the door, but as ever he waits patiently just outside even though he's quivering to get away.

I hold on to the hat rack as I push both feet into my rubber boots. I've pulled my thick socks up high over my tracksuit bottoms to keep them from riding up.

The minute I've closed the door behind me, Sixten speeds off towards the woods behind the house. I follow him as he makes his way among the trees that help to shield the house from the wind.

*8.20 a.m.*

*House empty when I arrive, no sign of Bo or Sixten.*
*Waited a while, but they haven't come back. Ingrid on way*
*over. Going out to look.*

*Johanna*

THE TRAIL is quite steep at first, flanked on both sides by bare branches and scrub. It must have rained overnight, because the twigs on the ground are slippery. My foot catches on a branch and I stumble, though luckily I manage to grab another one higher up to stop myself from falling.

Sixten is already down in the meadow. It's my favourite place, the wildflowers like a natural bouquet surrounded by trees.

'Bring me some flowers,' you often said when I grabbed the lead and let the dogs out. 'If you're heading down to the meadow, that is,' you added, though you knew I almost always did.

'Compliments of the florist,' I used to say when I got back, proudly holding the big bunch of blooms out to you.

You would put them down on the kitchen counter and carefully trim the stems. Arrange them nicely in a vase on the table, usually the one your aunt gave us when we got married.

I pause by the edge of the meadow to catch my breath. I've been here so many times over the years, whenever I've been tired or needed to think. After Hans announced that he'd joined the Young Conservatives, for example. Or when Ture got sick for the first time. After you left home for the last time. I've always headed down here with the hound and just sat for a while. It probably doesn't change anything or leave me any the wiser, but I like to think that it makes the hum inside me ease off a little.

The leaves of the aspen in the middle of the meadow rustle in the breeze. The neighbours' lad spotted a young bear at the top of one of the spruces when he came down here with his dog a few years back.

'He must've lost his mum,' the boy explained. 'He was just sitting there, crying for her.'

I already knew there were lots of bears in the woods that year, because Blixten had been sticking close to me for days, his tail between his legs. You just shrugged, weren't the least bit bothered or afraid, but Ture refused to visit that autumn.

'I bet you anything I'd be the first person to be killed by a bear since 1989,' he said, shaking his head when I asked if he wanted to go mushroom picking.

They shot the young bear a year later. Without its mother, it started going too close to the houses in search of food. The bear was cute enough as a cub, but no one wanted a full-grown male sniffing about in their yard.

I gaze out at the sea of flowers. Blue, white, yellow and green. Clover, harebell and the magnificent big orange ones, too.

I can't see Sixten, but the flowers and grass sway in the distance as he runs through them. Like a whirlwind blowing its way across the meadow.

They'll cut it all back soon, bale it up ahead of winter. Once that happens, you can be sure the autumn colours are coming, that the aspen on the edge of the glade will soon turn red.

If you were here, you would have picked a bouquet, said that you might as well.

My legs feel strong, so I decide to do a lap of the meadow, down on to the old forest track and then up on to the main road past the mailboxes. It isn't too far, but there are a few ups and downs.

I'm glad I don't have a nappy on, because it makes me feel more agile, my feet lighter. I speed up as I try to work out where Sixten is, pinecones crunching underfoot. There are a lot of them this year. Sixten comes running towards me with a stick, but he stops a few metres away. He's the only one of my dogs who has ever done this. He wants me to throw things for him, but he never brings them back; I have to find replacements instead. I tried to teach him to fetch as a pup, but it was hopeless.

My joints feel stiff as I bend down to pick up a stick, and I have to make a real effort to reach it. I throw it as hard as I can, and Sixten sets off after it. Just before he reaches the stick, he leaps forward and jumps on top of it. Grabs it in his mouth and swings his head from side to side as though it's a catch he needs to kill. I like his enthusiasm. After a moment or two, he lies down and starts gnawing at it instead. I pick up another and hurl it away.

It's July, but the wind is cold, and the air feels a little nippy. I speed up again in an attempt to warm myself up. I normally walk with my eyes on the ground to watch where I'm stepping, but I'm distracted by Sixten, who has raced off again towards the trees. Follow him in hunting mode as he trots along with his nose to the ground, sniffing the mice's trails.

It happens so quickly that I don't have time to break my fall. Just like that, I'm lying with my face on the ground, the smell of damp forest filling my nostrils. If I had my glasses on, I'd be able to see the ants marching in front of me. Without them, they're nothing but coloured blurs, but I know there is a hill right beside me. It's been there since Hans was a boy.

My knee feels tender, but other than that I'm not in any more pain than usual. I roll over on to my side and manage to sit up. Hadn't noticed the fallen tree trunk that has become an overgrown mound.

Sixten runs over to me and starts licking my face, whimpering.

'Hey, hey, it's OK,' I mutter, crawling over to one of the aspen trees.

I lean against it and close my eyes. My knee is hurting more now, and the strength that was just pulsing through me has vanished. The wind stirs the leaves, making the hair on my arms stand on end. Sixten pricks his ears and sits down around a metre away from me, gazing out across the meadow. He is without doubt the wimpiest dog I've ever owned, but I have no idea what he'd do in the face of real danger. The wimpiest could be the ones who rise to the occasion when push comes to shove.

'I just need to have a little rest,' I mumble, tipping my head back against the trunk.

*12.30 p.m.*

*Sixten was loose, running around by the meadow where we found Bo leaning against a tree, slightly confused. Had wet himself. Says he's fine, but doesn't really know how he ended up there. Showered and in clean clothes. Ingrid will write a report and contact Hans.*

*Johanna & Ingrid*

THE SHOWER actually did me a lot of good. Johanna was so firm that I couldn't say no.

'It's non-negotiable,' she said, turning on her heel and marching into the bathroom to put on her apron and gloves.

I didn't notice how cold I was while I was down at the meadow, but by the time I got home I was chilled to the bone. Johanna scrubbed me until my skin was red. Washed my hair and beard without a word of argument from me. She then got me into a clean pair of tracksuit bottoms and a shirt, and I'd let her put on a nappy without protest, even thought it felt good to be tucked up in bed.

I turn my head, first to the left and then the right. The new bed feels like an ocean, and I can't believe a person could possibly need this much space to sleep. Hans went on and on about how great it is, but I find the whole contraption stupid and awkward. I fiddle with the remote control. They called it an 'adapted' bed, but I have no idea who this damn thing was adapted for, because it sure as hell wasn't me. Hans and the man from Assistive Services both showed me how to raise one end of it, but I can't remember what they said. I reach for the cup of tea on the bedside table and take a sip instead.

Johanna and Ingrid are busy flicking through a file of papers at the far side of the kitchen. Ingrid says something, and Johanna nods solemnly.

'I'll finish up here,' says Ingrid. 'Marie said she'd cover MA and TE for me, so I don't have any more stops to make.'

'OK,' says Johanna, giving her a thumbs-up.

She goes out into the hallway, puts on her trainers and grabs her fleece. When she is ready to go, she pops her head back into the kitchen.

'Bye, Bo. Make sure you stay inside now, OK?' she tells me. 'I don't want to find you down by the meadow again.'

As though it's my fault I fell and got stuck there.

'Yes, yes,' I mutter.

The room is quiet once Johanna is gone. Ingrid is still reading through the file. After a moment or two, she closes it and clutches it to her stomach. Turns towards me without a word. I feel uneasy, don't know why she is being so quiet.

Sixten gets up from the floor and trots over to her, presses his nose between her thighs. He wants her to scratch him behind both ears.

Ingrid's fingers dig into his coat as her eyes drift out through the window.

'You know we'll have to write a report about this, don't you, Bo?' she says.

'Report,' I snort, though what I really want is to shout the way my old man did when I got lazy about the woodpile and the whole thing came crashing down.

I was just taking my damn dog for a walk in the woods. The same woods I'd been exploring for half a century before any of these people were even a twinkle in their old man's eye. I want to say all of that, but all I can manage is yet another:

'Report?'

Ingrid comes over to the bed and pats the foot of the mattress. Sixten looks up at me and then turns to her. She nods. He jumps up and lies flat out beside my legs, and I immediately feel a little better.

'I'll do my best to explain that there were extenuating circumstances,' she says, making air quotes with her fingers as she says 'extenuating'. 'But this could have been really bad, you know that.'

I take a deep breath, ready to argue, but the words won't come out. Instead, all I can manage is an empty sigh. I don't know what 'really bad' even means any more.

My eyes are stinging, so I close them for a moment. Ingrid pours a glass of water and leaves it with an energy drink on the little nightstand by my bed. They took the kitchen table away too.

'I'll get you some chocolate,' she says.

I hear the rustling as she opens the wrapper, and I mumble thanks with my eyes still closed, one hand on Sixten's back. He is already breathing heavily.

Sleep takes over, making everything better.

'You get some rest now, Bo, and I'll see you tomorrow. I'm working the day shift, so I'll take Sixten out.'

Yes, yes, I think, but I'm already miles away when Ingrid closes the door.

*6.30 p.m.*

*Bo seems brighter. Fried sausage and mash. Took Sixten
out to do his business and for a dip in the stream.*

*Kalle*

THE RINGING is so shrill, but at first I can't find my phone. It's on a shelf beneath the bedside table, and the mattress is so soft that it's tricky to hold my upper body up when I try to reach it. My elbows sink in, and my arms start to shake, but eventually I manage to get hold of the phone and slump back against the pillows. *Ellinor*, I read on the screen, feeling a flutter of excitement. I clear my throat.

'Yes, hello, Bo Andersson speaking.'

'Grandad, are you OK?' She sounds anxious.

Her voice flicks some sort of switch in my chest, and it feels like I'm about to start crying, but instead I swallow.

'Dad just called and said that the carers found you in the woods?' she says, before I have time to speak. 'That you'd fallen while you were out with Sixten?'

'Ah, yes,' I reply, laughing though I'm not sure why. 'We were just out for a walk, but I took a bit of a tumble.' I add the last part in an attempt not to seem completely useless.

Ellinor sighs.

'I didn't hurt myself or anything, so there's no need to worry.'

'Of course I'm worried! You could have broken a bone and been stuck out there.'

No one seems to be worried about me being stuck here in this hospital bed, I think, accidentally glaring at Sixten, who gives a small whine.

There is a rustling on the line, and I guess Ellinor must have moved her phone over to her other ear. I force myself up, so that I'm sitting on the edge of the bed.

'Sorry, I know you like going out with Sixten,' she says after a moment. 'I just get so worried. We all do. Dad was really worried when he called. I could hear it in his voice.'

'Hans? Worried? I doubt that,' I snort.

'Of course he was. He just has trouble showing it.'

How hard can it be to tell the truth, I wonder, clearing my throat.

I listen to the sound of Ellinor breathing, and feel a sudden urge for her to tell me more about Hans. I want her to explain why he is the way he is, why he's such hard work.

'Mmm,' I say, stroking Sixten's head. 'How is everything at university, then?'

'It's also the case that you're not the best at realizing when he's worried, too,' she says, ignoring my question. 'Or that we worry because we love you, simple as that.' For some reason, she says the last part in English.

My face grows hot. There are times when she knows more about me than I know about myself, and it's both thrilling and uncomfortable to hear her confidently lay out exactly what I'm like and how I feel.

'You know how it is, bumblebee,' I say. 'Life's not easy.'

'Hmm.'

'Come on, then. How is university?' I ask again, jotting down *English?* on the scrap of paper in front of me. I'll have to ask Ture what he makes of youngsters using so much English these days.

Ellinor tells me all about the course books she has ordered ahead of the autumn term, and I never want her to stop. She sounds so excited as she takes me through the different theories on how to talk to people.

'Oh?' I say. I wonder what's really in those books.

She has done two terms, she explains. And right now she is doing a summer placement at a home for people who can't take care of themselves.

'I'll come to visit soon, though,' she says. 'Sofie might come too. Do you remember her? You met her last Christmas.'

'Of course. That'll be nice,' I say, though I don't remember. Hans almost never brought any of his classmates home with him, but Ellinor often brings friends to see me.

'How's Sixten doing?' she asks, which makes me wonder whether her dad has shared his demented plans with her. I'm not sure whether we talked about Sixten the last time she was here.

'He's fine, stretched out here beside me,' I say, giving him a pat on the head.

'I know it must be getting harder,' she says. 'To look after him, I mean.'

'Oh, it's no problem for me. Hans is the only one who seems to find it tricky,' I say, feeling irritated.

'Mmm.'

Ellinor moves her phone over to the other ear again. We sit quietly for a while, trying to think of something to say.

'I can help you clip his claws when I come over,' she says after a moment, and I smile at the thought of Ellinor and Sixten on the kitchen floor in front of me.

'Please. I'd like that,' I say, suddenly feeling more hopeful.

Ellinor won't let Hans take him. She'll make sure he stays right here where he belongs.

# Saturday
# 22 July

I ADD a little more lubricant to the chain and then set the pot down on the ground. Turn the pedals to make sure it's evenly spread. I've had the bike for two weeks, and the sturdy tyres make it feel like I'm flying down the snowy roads. It takes me less than ten minutes to get to Krokom now. I turn the Monark the right way up again, wipe down the frame with a clean cloth, and brush the snow from the handlebars. Wheel it over to the front door and then take a step back to admire it. Decide to push it a little further, leaning it against the wall rather than using the kickstand.

I dry my hands and shove the rag in my pocket. The cold air nips at my fingers as I make my way over to the storehouse to grab the gravel bucket, sprinkling more of it on to the path outside the block of workers' rooms – don't want Mother to slip and fall now that they're finally coming to visit. I kick the snow from my boots by the door, then head inside to find some soap and get cleaned up. You're humming to yourself by the sink. I pour in some luke-warm water from the tub by the stove and move over beside you. You rest your head on my shoulder for a moment, and I breathe in your scent, can't get enough of it.

'There, that's the last one,' you say, putting the lid on the pot and lifting it on to the stove.

You add one more log to the fire and carry the empty holder over to the door. Pull my woollen sweater over your head and go out to fetch more wood.

I wash, let my hands drip for a moment, then dry them on the tea towel. I think about how clean the room is. I hang up the towel and trail a finger along the top of the skirting board, but there isn't a speck of dirt. You even helped me hem the curtains with an embroidered edge, the way I know Mother likes them.

My eyes come to rest on the door frame, and I decide to add another nail to the corner. It's better, but the gap is still there; the wall behind it has bowed outwards.

It's been six months since I packed my bag and walked down to the road, to catch the bus to Östersund and then Krokom. From there, I walked the rest of the way to Hissmofors.

'Right, I'm off,' I said, as I picked up my bag in the porch at home. I glanced over to my old man, who was looking down at the paper, but he didn't move a muscle.

'Bo is leaving now, Lars-Erik,' said Mother.

He lifted his head and grunted.

'Ta-ra, then,' he said, before looking down again.

I nodded and made my way outside. Crouched down in front of the dogs and stroked their backs. Mother tied a shawl beneath her chin and walked me to the bus stop. We strapped my bag to the pannier rack of my father's bike and pushed it between us.

'It'll be good, this,' she said, her eyes on the ground.

'It'll be good,' I repeated, pointing over to the avenue of birches outside Evertsson's place. The leaves had started to turn yellow. 'Look. So pretty.'

She followed my eyes and smiled. Autumn was her favourite time of year. The colours, the mushrooms, the harvest.

'The house'll feel empty, though,' she said, pursing her lips.

I would miss Mother, I knew that, but I was also so excited about everything that awaited me that I hadn't really given it much thought. Still, my footsteps grew heavier the closer to the bus stop we came.

I tug at the edge of the curtain. Want you to feel as welcomed by my family as I do by yours.

'Father isn't one to get angry, no,' you told me one Sunday afternoon, as we walked back to my place after lunch with your little sister. I had asked whether your old man ever lost his temper.

I remember being amazed, wondering how that was even possible, how you could never have seen him lose his rag. Maybe it had something to do with the drink, with the fact that your father didn't touch the stuff, because my old man was always worse after a few bottles.

You come back in and take your gloves off, head straight over to the stove to get some heat into your rosy fingers. Though you still live with your parents, you've made yourself at home here with me.

'It'll be just fine, you'll see. I'm looking forward to meeting your parents. And it's only lunch,' you say, pressing your hands to my cheeks. Your palms are nice and cool.

I gaze into your eyes for a moment. It feels absurd that someone as beautiful as you would want to be with someone like me. The ice on your lashes has melted, and I reach up to wipe some moisture from your eyelids.

'Shall we go, then?' you ask, letting go of my face.


The exhaust coughs out dark smoke as the bus pulls away, small clouds of hot breath hanging in the air around the passengers' heads. There aren't many of them, and I spot my old man right away, towering above the others. Mother is a few metres behind him, and I'm struck by how old she looks.

It isn't something I normally do, but as my father approaches, I take off my cap and nod in greeting.

'Bo, dear,' says Mother, speeding up and moving in front of him to reach me. She takes off her gloves and cups my cheeks the way you just did, then quickly glances in your direction.

'And this must be young Fredrika, I take it?'

You smile and curtsey, and Mother gives you a hug.

'Good day, Miss,' my old man says, and his words send a wave of relief through my gut.

We walk slowly back to my room, you and Mother talking about Hissmofors and your family. My father and I are on either side of you, and I say a few words from time to time, but mostly we just walk in silence, glad that the two of you seem to be getting on so well.

'Gosh, how lovely. Is that yours, Bo?' Mother blurts out when she spots the bicycle. 'Have you seen, Lars-Erik?'

I can't help but smile as he lumbers over to the Monark and runs a finger over the frame. It looks like he is about to say something, but then he closes his mouth, turns around and gazes back along the road.

'See you've got electricity out here, then,' he says finally, stroking his chin. 'You've got the power station.'

Mother nods and looks up at the cables. You hook your arm through mine and smile at her.

'Come on, let's get inside where it's warm. I've already laid the table for us,' you say, pulling me towards the door.

My room is towards the far end of the building. Each of us workers has our own space, and we share an outhouse in the yard. The room is quite big, but we'll have to find somewhere bigger when we're living together.

It's cramped at the table, which wasn't made for any more than two. Mother asks if you've ever seen an electric stove, and you tell her that I'm having one fitted soon. She raises an eyebrow at that, impressed, and I glance over to my old man, who looks around the room without a word.

Silence settles over us, and I try to come up with something to say, but I'm too tired. Struggled to sleep last night, tossing and turning until well after midnight. Mother praises your food, and I tell them that the meat came from your parents. The spuds, too.

'There's a gap up there. You need to attach the frame better,' says my old man, gesturing up at the corner of the doorway.

You give me a quick glance, then get up to fetch the water jug. You ask Mother if she wants any, then fill her glass to the brim. I try to tell myself that I don't care what he thinks, that the most important thing is that you and Mother get on and that he doesn't lose his temper, but disappointment still digs its claws into me. I would have liked to tell him about my work at the sawmill, how it differs from the mill in Ranviken, but he doesn't ask.

When we've all finished eating, I lower my cutlery to the plate and get up.

'We should probably get going so you don't miss your bus,' I say. Mother looks down.

Dusk has started to fall outside, and we're almost at the bus station when you announce that you're going to head home. You curtsey politely and say it was nice to meet them. My old man lifts his cap and then turns and keeps walking.

Mother presses a hand to my cheek again. She looks like she is about to say something, but then quickly pulls back and hurries after him.

I lift a hand and wave, watching you get smaller and smaller. I want to run after you, but am interrupted by the sound of knocking. I shake my head and turn around to see where my parents are, but the road and the bus have gone. The knocking starts again. I open my eyes and stare up at the ceiling for a moment, can still feel the December chill in the air.

I rub my face and cough.

Sixten shuffles higher up the bed and lowers his head to my belly. I meet his eye and stroke his head.

'Come in, then.'

10 a.m.

*Here to visit. Restocked the freezer. There's a new pack of toilet roll by the back door, cream cakes in the fridge. The bags of wood are in the porch. Talked about Sixten, didn't quite see eye to eye. Dad isn't in the right mood.*

*Hans*

HE'S GOING to use the fall in the woods against me, as a way to boost his argument. To prove that he has the right to take Sixten away.

Hans is on a chair beside my bed, his eyes on the picture of you on the nightstand, and the rasping sound from his nervous hand on his stubbly chin is really grating on me.

I know what he's going to say. He's been mulling it over for a while now, fine-tuning the argument in his head, and has finally plucked up the courage to get started.

'This can't go on, Dad. You know that as well as I do,' he says, as though he still hasn't realized this is war. That it's his will against mine. That he's the one who gets to decide.

I don't know when it happened, but we've switched roles. He has never come close to being as big or strong as I was, but he has all the authority now. He's the one in charge of my life. I'm the reason he's even alive, but I'm also the one who has to bow down to him. Who depends on his decisions. He's the person people listen to, not me.

No one listens to me the way they listened to my old man. Right down to the last, people did exactly what he wanted.

I try to fight it, but my eyes well up all the same. I don't want him to see, so I close them. Pretend I'm tired. There's no way in hell I'm giving him this.

'Sixten is suffering here; you can't take care of him. There's no other choice,' he continues with a sigh.

Beside me, Sixten stirs. Lifts his head and yawns.

A sudden panic grips me. Any anger I felt fades away, and all that's left is fear. It feels like our son has his hands around my throat, like he's squeezing as hard as he can.

What if I give up my Tuesday shower or a couple of morning coffees, I want to ask. Won't they have time to take him out then?

'It's not the carers' job to look after people's pets.' He says it so quickly that it sounds rehearsed, a point I can't argue with.

'What about Marita?' I ask instead, clearing my throat. 'Maybe she could come over to take him out from time to time?'

Hans shakes his head.

Anger surges through me again, and I feel like throwing my hot tea in his face. Screaming that this sure as hell isn't how I raised my son to behave.

I can't quite read the look on his face, but I think I can see something unhappy there and that makes me furious. What right does *he* have to be unhappy when he could stop this madness right now? He's acting like the decision is out of his hands, like someone is forcing him to take Sixten away from me.

I meet his gaze. This isn't right, I want to say, you don't split a flock.

We've argued so many times, but today all I feel is emptiness.

'This is how it's going to be,' he says, getting to his feet. I haven't complained or said a word against it, but he adds: 'And that's that.'

My throat is oddly tight, and I wish you were here. That, in your role as his mother, you could put an admonishing hand on his shoulder. A rebuke, a warning, letting him know that this is no way to treat his father. That there has to be a line somewhere. It didn't matter how awful my old man was, I knew my place.

Sixten lowers his head to my belly and closes his eyes again. The tightness in my throat gets even worse, and I feel dizzy.

Someone else will take care of Sixten. Someone other than me. But I'm the only one who knows how he likes his ears squeezed.

*12.30 p.m.*

*Potatoes with fish balls in sauce. Bo had a visit from Hans this morning. It's been decided that Sixten will be moving, and Bo isn't happy. I put his food on the bedside table, but Bo didn't want any.*

*Ingrid*

I DON'T want to do anything. Nothing but lie here in this damn bed, waiting for something to change. Or maybe I'm waiting for it all to be over. The whole lot.

My vision grows hazy, and I see you coming towards me. Sleep is even more of a sanctuary than usual.

'What do we need?' you ask, even though you're the one with the shopping list in your pocket.

I don't speak. As ever, I just wait for you to tell me instead.

'Milk, butter and fermented milk,' you say, and with that I trudge off to the shop. 'Just one of each,' you call after me.

We're going to stay with your parents next week, which means the house will be empty for a while. As ever, I'm taking all of my holiday in one go, and you and Hans will be there all summer.

'I'll be spending my summers in Hissmofors, just so you know,' you told me, after we found out I'd inherited the house in Renäs.

I can still feel the cool weight of the milk carton in my hand when Sixten stretches, his back pressing up against my side.

'It's just not the same without them,' you said, when I asked whether you missed Hissmofors.

I didn't understand it at the time, but now I think I know what you meant. Now that I'm lying in a strange bed in a kitchen without you. Now that Sixten is going to be taken away from me.

A ringing sound cuts through the room. Sixten pushes his nose beneath my elbow and gives me a gentle nudge, and all thoughts of your family fade away. But the idea that you probably under-stood more about life than I ever did stays with me.

The ringing starts again, and I pick up my phone. *Hans*, it says on the screen.

'I don't bloody think so,' I mutter, putting it back down and leaving it to ring. 'You can go to hell.'

I close my eyes and wait for the noise to stop. If I ignore him, he'll change his mind. He'll realize he's making a huge mistake.

The ringing stops, and I open my eyes. Reach for the phone and press the green button, followed by *Ture*.

*5.45 p.m.*

*Fish balls still on the table, re-heated them. Tried to tempt Bo to eat. He's not interested. Says several times he's not going to let Sixten go.*

*Kalle*

# Sunday
# 23 July

*7.40 a.m.*

*Bo in bed, seems a little out of sorts. Wanted porridge
for breakfast. Reminded him to blow into the bottle.
Warm day today, important he drinks plenty of fluids.
Medication.*

*Johanna*

MY BODY feels heavy. Heavier than usual. I sway as I'm about to sit down on the edge of the bed. It's so soft that it's tricky to keep my balance.

Sixten jumps down to the floor and trots over to his water bowl for a drink. I find it hard to look at him without my eyes welling up.

I grab my phone and switch it to loudspeaker. One ring after another echoes through the quiet kitchen, but Ture doesn't pick up.

Still gripping the mobile, my hand slides down to my knee. I sit there, just waiting for him to call me back, but he doesn't.

Sixten licks his chops, catching the droplets of water that are clinging to the fur around his mouth before walking back over to me and resting his head on my thigh. His water bowl is empty, I notice. I'll have to remember to fill it up later.

I try again. The phone rings and rings, but Ture still doesn't answer. My heart starts racing, and I break out in a cold sweat as my brain immediately goes to the worst-case scenario: Ture unconscious on the bathroom floor.

I remember a conversation we had a few years back, about where we want to be buried.

'Not in some random bloody churchyard in town, that's for sure,' he said. 'And not in Hissmofors either, for that matter.'

We were sitting by the big chessboard in the park at the time, waiting for our turn. Ture always won, but I enjoyed playing against him all the same.

'I'll be in Hissmofors, beside Fredrika,' I said.

You were clear on that point, that that was where you wanted to rest, as you put it. And since it didn't really matter to me, I promised you that would be what happened.

'You can take my place by Sundy Church if you want,' I said, holding out another mazarin to Ture.

He looked up at me, as though he were trying to work out whether I was joking or not. I thought he took the whole funeral thing a bit too seriously, considering he wasn't even religious.

He sat quietly for a while.

'I suppose the memorial garden in Sundy will do for me,' he said with a firm nod. 'No grave, no headstone. Just a little plaque.'

I wait a few minutes, then press the green button again. Sixten has lain down on the floor, where it's a little cooler.

There is a click on the other end of the line, and I feel the tightness around my heart ease slightly.

'Hi,' Ture says, in a voice that sounds about as heavy as I feel.

'Hi, how're things?' I ask.

Ture doesn't speak, and fear grips me again.

'Hello, are you still there?'

He sighs.

'It's all gone to shit,' he says after a moment, so bluntly that I'm surprised.

Ture is someone who has always asked direct questions, the kind I'm powerless against, but he rarely answers with the same openness.

'Same here,' I say, because there really isn't any other way to put it.

We sit quietly for a while.

'About as bloody fucking awful as they can be,' he says.

'Mmm,' I reply, noticing that Sixten has dozed off.

'It's strange,' Ture goes on, exhaling so deeply that it makes the line crackle. 'Don't you think it's funny how they've got us clinging on to life?'

'Yeah.'

This is something we've talked about quite a bit, that we don't want to go on living if we don't have any life left in us.

'But then the doc says there's nothing he can do, and all I want is for him to fix it,' Ture continues, and I remember that he had an appointment this week.

'That bad?'

'That bad.'

We let the clocks tick for a moment or two.

'All I really have left is you and these chats,' he says eventually. 'So I guess it's my time.'

I've never really thought about that before, whether he wanted a family. Always took it for granted that he didn't. He would've been a good dad – probably much better than me. He's got the patience for it.

'Maybe it is,' I say.

He is quiet on the other end of the line. I'm on the verge of telling him that things could be worse. That it could be Per-Olof he has to talk to every week, our old colleague from the mill, a difficult bastard. But I make myself hold back. Know I shouldn't joke about something like this.

'How do you feel, then?' I ask instead, though what I really want is to talk shit about Per-Olof.

He takes a deep, trembling breath.

'Fucking awful,' he says. 'But it is what it is, you know?'

Our clocks are ticking out of sync, and I want to make everything better. To do something to make it all easier.

I called him after you left, and I wish I could say something now that would help him the way he helped me, but I can't remember what he said. All I remember is how it felt, that the weight on my chest lifted.

'That's it. It is what it is,' I say, moving my phone over to my other hand.

I try to think of something less heavy to talk about, something that'll cheer him up but which doesn't sound flippant.

'At least you've travelled a lot. I've barely left Jämtland,' I say.

Oh, I've been jealous of his trips over the years. The shorter ones, to Gothenburg, but also when he left the country. I'd probably never admit it out loud, but I would never have been able to leave like that.

'I've seen a lot, I have,' Ture replies, and I think his voice does sound a little brighter.

'All those stories you told me. Sometimes it feels as if I was right there with you.'

He laughs.

'Oh yeah?'

'It is what it is, you know?' I say again, though the words stick in my throat. 'And it'll happen when it happens.'

'I guess it will,' he says, letting out a deep sigh.

*2.10 p.m.*

*Bo says he's not hungry, but the rice pudding with sugar still goes down a treat. Hans here. Warm today, but not too warm for a fire, according to Bo. Took Sixten for a walk and filled his water bowl, which was empty.*

*Ingrid*

I WAKE to the sound of Hans and Ingrid chatting in the kitchen, hadn't realized Hans was here. They're hunched over the work-top, looking at whatever Ingrid is holding.

'Good nap?' Ingrid asks, nudging her glasses down on to the tip of her nose.

'Yes, thanks,' I reply with a yawn.

Sixten wakes and stretches. He's used to the new bed now.

Ingrid pushes her glasses back into place and looks down at the object in her hands.

'I remember that evening well,' Hans tells her, his face cracking into a smile.

He seems moved, which makes me curious about what they could be looking at.

'I've heard good things about youth theatre, that they get to try out all sorts there. My sister's kids were crazy about it,' she says.

'It was fun for the old folks too,' Hans replies, nodding to me. 'The grandparents often went along with the kids.'

Where did I go, I want to ask, but I have to yawn again.

'We found these lovely pictures, Bo. Of Ellinor playing a bumblebee in the school play,' Ingrid explains, holding up one of the photographs. 'They were in the bedroom.'

The picture is the one of me holding Ellinor Bee's hand fifteen years ago, and I remember that I had been planning to give them to Hans.

'She was so funny on stage, wasn't she, Dad? Playing a bee that was too fat to fly, do you remember?'

I do, and I can't help but laugh.

Ingrid watches us both, and we laugh even more. Sixten's head bobs up and down on my belly.

'I wanted you to have that,' I say, once the laughter peters out. 'The one of me and our bee outside the school.'

'Oh?' says Hans.

'I found it in one of the boxes, thought you might want it,' I say, stroking Sixten's head. 'As a memory.'

He clears his throat.

'Thanks. That's nice of you.'

Ingrid takes off her glasses and perches them on top of her head. She smiles at me.

'That was sweet of you, Bo,' she says, glancing over at Hans. 'Pictures are great things to have.'

Silence fills the kitchen, and I don't know what else to say. I just stroke Sixten's head and look up at our son.

'Do you want me to keep the fire going?' Ingrid asks after a moment.

I nod, and she adds another couple of logs, then starts tidying the kitchen.

'Shall I show you what I chucked in the freezer?' Hans asks. 'Before I head off.'

'May as well,' Ingrid replies, making her way through to the porch and shoving her feet into her trainers.

Hans pushes his hair back and pulls on his cap. He looks as if he wants to say something, but nothing comes out.

'OK. Bye, then,' he says, still staring at me.

'Bye.'

'And thanks for this.' He holds up the picture of me and Ellinor Bee. 'It's really great.'

I feel the corners of my mouth twitch, and I look down at my hands.

'You're welcome.'

The door swings shut behind him, and I feel calm. But then Sixten pushes up against my legs, and I remember that he is going to be taken away from me.

# Wednesday
# 2 August

I'M READY and waiting in the porch when Hans pulls up on the driveway. He called as he left town to let me know he was coming for Sixten. The car door opens, and he slowly gets out of the driver's seat.

I glare at him through the window and then turn the gold lock. There's no way in hell he's going to take him. Not today.

Hans closes the car door and turns to face the house. He takes off his cap and runs a hand over his forehead and hair. Squeezes his earlobe, massaging it with his fingers, then stands perfectly still with his eyes on the gravel.

Anger surges up inside me. I grab one of the logs from the bags on the bench and grip it as hard as I can. The sun is shining in through the window, which means the porch is warm even though it's still early. A couple of flies bounce against the pane of glass, buzzing stubbornly. The air smells stale, and I'm sweaty.

I put the log back in the bag and make my way through to my bed, lying down beside Sixten to wait. I hear the first tug on the door handle a few seconds later.

'Have you locked the door?' Hans calls from the other side, tugging on the handle again. 'What the hell?'

Did he really think it would be that easy? That he could just walk in here and take him?

'You're not going anywhere,' I say, stroking Sixten's head.

Hans is quiet outside, and for a split second I think he must have gone. That he's seen sense at last. Who knows, maybe he's ashamed of himself and will call later to apologize.

I get up to check. Through the kitchen window, I see him fiddling with his phone. He looks up and I take a quick step to one side, but it's too late.

Hans marches over to the kitchen window and pounds on it with his fist. The glass rattles in its frame.

'For God's sake, Dad. Open the door!'

I press back against the wall as hard as I can so that he won't be able to see me. The shadow of his head moves across the side of the stove. From where he is lying on the bed, Sixten lifts his head and gives me a confused look.

'Don't make me call Ingrid to ask for the spare key,' Hans shouts, his forehead against the glass.

I feel an urge to giggle and have to clamp a hand to my mouth.

'What the hell,' Hans mutters again, just as his shadow disappears from the fireplace.

Has he gone this time? Sixten crawls down to the foot of the bed so that I can stroke him.

'Hiya, Ingrid, how's it going? It's me, Hans. Bo Andersson's son.'

I peer out through the window and see Hans wandering towards your old vegetable patch with his phone to his ear.

As quietly as I can, I undo the latch and open the window a few centimetres, so I can hear better.

'No, nothing has happened. He's fine. Hiding from me in the kitchen and refusing to let me in.' Hans kicks at a dandelion that is growing in one of the long-neglected beds. 'OK, how long will that take?'

He sighs and rubs his face. I turn around and grin at Sixten.

'I think she's messing with him,' I whisper.

'The thing is, I've got a meeting at ten and—' Ingrid must have interrupted him because he stops talking. 'Yes, of course, I understand that. I'll wait here until you arrive,' he says after a moment or two, in a more conciliatory tone. 'Thanks, Ingrid.'

The minute he ends the call, he looks up at the kitchen window, and I close it as quickly as I can. He turns his head and peers over at the forest, his hands hanging by his sides. As though he might find the answers he's looking for there.

Right then, out of nowhere, it starts to rain. Drumming down on the tin roof. I peer out and see Hans running towards his car, and the giggles bubble up inside me again.

I walk over to the fridge and break off a piece of chocolate, pop it into my mouth and then stretch out on the bed beside Sixten, who presses up against me.


We both wake to three loud knocks on the door, followed by Hans's voice.

'Ingrid is here now, Dad. She's going to let me in.'

I glance up at the clock. We must have been asleep for at least a couple of hours.

I hear a clicking sound as the lock turns, and I break out in a cold sweat, feel queasy.

A frowning Hans pops his head in from the porch. He's dripping wet from the rain.

'I need the loo,' he says, stomping across the kitchen floor.

Ingrid follows him in.

'Hi, Bo.' Her smile seems uncomfortable. 'I'm sorry. I tried to drag it out.'

I scratch Sixten's neck, but I don't speak.

'Good work, anyway,' she says, glancing over towards the bathroom, where Hans has just flushed. 'I really mean it.'

I shrug.

'I've got to get going now – you know how it is – but I'll be back again tomorrow.'

She puts a hand on my shoulder, hesitates, but then says nothing. Then eventually she gives my shoulder a squeeze.

'I'm sorry,' she says again.

When Hans comes back into the kitchen, Ingrid fixes her eyes on him. I might be imagining things, but I think I see them narrow as she releases my shoulder and leaves.

Hans shakes his head as the door clicks shut behind her.

'Dad . . .' he begins.

I glare at him, and he sighs and kicks off his shoes with such force that Sixten flinches. As though he has any right to vent his anger, as though he has the right to be angry at all.

If you were here, you'd talk him round. You would come through from the sewing room and give him that look of yours that says enough is enough. The one he's always listened to, in a way he's never listened to me.

But you aren't here, and nothing matters any more.

Sixten curls up beside me, nudging my sausage fingers with his nose. He doesn't want this. I don't want this. But it doesn't matter what either of us wants. That stopped mattering a long time ago.

'He's going to be so happy. There are even kids in the family,' Hans says, but the look on his face tells me that he knows how immoral this is, what he is about to do.

I'm stretched out on an overly soft bed that belongs to the local authority with Sixten by my side, and all I can feel for our son is disdain. I can tell just by looking at him how weak and pathetic he thinks I am. He isn't even gearing up for a fight; he feels sorry for me. But he won't show mercy. Despite my weakness, he'll leave me bloody and bruised.

Our son fumbles with the lead. The clip gets caught on the hook, and he tugs it loose. His aftershave makes my nose sting.

'Come on, Sixten, time for a walk,' he says in a babyish voice, once he has finally managed to get to grips with the collar and lead.

But Sixten doesn't budge from my side, and he doesn't look up at Hans.

Hans shakes the lead again, and images of Buster race through my mind. That's when the dizziness and nausea get worse.

'It's the only way,' my father grunted once the neighbour had left.

Buster had been out of sorts for the past few days, limping and refusing to eat, but my old man didn't think it was worth taking him to the vet. Not when the neighbour knew so much about canines.

I was sitting in front of the stove, had just added more wood, and when I turned to Mother I thought I could see something sad in her eyes.

My father headed outside, and I crept over to Buster. He lifted his head and shuffled closer to me.

The door swung open, and Buster flinched. My old man had the gun slung over his shoulder, and he was wearing his boots.

'Just hold on, Lars-Erik. Give the boy a chance to say goodbye first.'

He snorted, but didn't argue. Just sat down on one of the kitchen chairs to wait.

I turned to Mother again.

'What do you mean?' I asked.

She wiped her hands on her skirt and looked away. Wrapped the bread in a cloth and set it down on the counter.

'It's time to say goodbye to Buster,' she said finally with a firm nod. 'That's just how it is.'

I patted Buster's head. Gave him a scratch beside the little flap on his ear, and he pressed up against my hand.

'Right, that's enough,' my old man snapped. He sounded stressed. 'He's got to learn at some point.'

With that, he took Buster and left. I looked up at Mother, still didn't understand what was happening, but she didn't explain. Just mumbled something about going out to check on the animals, even though the milking was already done. The minute she had closed the door behind her, I put on my boots and my jacket.

The air felt raw, must have been below zero overnight. I was anxious, needed to find Buster and my old man, and so I sped up. Took the first trail to the right, then right again after the stream.

Glanced back over my shoulder as I ran across the bridge, even though it was far too cold to swim.

Right then, I heard my father's voice between the trees up ahead. 'Off you go, search.'

I ducked behind a juniper bush. The sharp needles clawed at my face.

That was when I spotted Buster, limping along with his nose to the ground. His skinny tail was in work mode, and I relaxed. They were just going hunting.

I slumped back on the ground. Buster, the most handsome foxhound I'd ever seen. Mother told me not to, but I thought of him as my big brother. He'd always taken care of me, always kept me company.

The shot that rang out was so loud that I clamped my hands over my ears. When I saw Buster's body on the ground, they flew to my mouth just as quickly.

My stomach churned and I threw up all the porridge I'd eaten earlier. It felt like someone had their hands around my throat, and I could barely breathe.

My old man was busy heaping earth on top of Buster, and he hadn't noticed me. The wind drowned out my tears.

I got up and started running back along the trail. I didn't know where I was going, just that I needed to get away. As far from him as I could be.

Sixten lifts his head from its hiding place beneath my hand and gives me a quick look. It makes my heart ache, because I know I can't help him, just like I couldn't help Buster.

When I brought Sixten home to live with us, I made him a promise that he could count on me. That I'd be there for him. But I've let him down.

He nudges his head beneath my hand again, and I desperately hope that he knows I didn't have a damn thing to do with this. That if it were down to me, he wouldn't be going anywhere. That he'd be able to stay by my side for as long as he wanted.

Hans shakes the lead again, and Sixten stares at me. I feel a tug in my chest, but I close my eyes and nod at him. Still, he doesn't get up. Doesn't take it as an order. Instead, his weight seems to get heavier on my legs, as though he's trying to cling on.

In the end, Hans comes towards us and loops the collar over his head. He pulls gently on it, and Sixten reluctantly hops down from the bed. I can't bring myself to look at him, so I keep my eyes closed.

Our son's hand is on my shoulder, but I don't move a muscle.

'I'm sorry, Dad, but this really is the only way,' he says. It sounds sincere, as though he is genuinely upset.

I screw up my eyes as tight as I can. Don't give a damn how he feels. Don't want to hear his voice. All I want is to feel Sixten's body against mine.


Once the door closes behind them, the silence digs its claws into me. Tears and snot pour down my cheeks, catching in my beard, and for a while it feels like I might actually suffocate. I gasp for air, but what I really want is to stop breathing.

*2 p.m.*

*Bosse in a mood, takes a while to get him into the shower.*
*Late for my next visit. Heated some fish gratin and left it*
*on the table.*

*Eva-Lena*

EVA-LENA IS pottering around the place, getting ready. She takes out a new protective apron and ties it around her waist. Pulls on some plastic gloves.

'OK then, time for your shower.'

I squeeze my eyes even more tightly shut, as though that might make her stroppy voice go away. If I just lie quietly, she might think I'm asleep and leave me alone.

'Come on, Bosse, wake up,' she says, shaking one of my legs.

I don't want to, but I open my eyes. They're still puffy and sore.

'If you sit up, I'll go and get everything ready in the bathroom. I don't have all the time in the world, you know,' she says, as she hurries out of the room.

Like hell.

My hand gropes for Sixten on the empty mattress beside me, and I feel like crying again.

I can hear Eva-Lena making a racket. Why is she here today? Which of the others is sick? My eyes sting, and I have to screw them up and take a deep breath to hold it all in. I wish Ingrid were here instead. Or Johanna, at the very least.

'Come on, Bosse. Are you still in bed?' Eva-Lena trudges over and grabs my shoulders. 'Let's get you up.'

'No,' I manage to stutter. 'I don't want to.'

My voice breaks, and I start coughing.

'This isn't about what you want. It's about what you need,' she says, pulling me upright and swinging my legs over the edge of the bed. She has me sitting up before I can even argue or fight back. 'Just look how dirty your beard is. It's full of food.'

There is something about her that makes me incapable of finding the right words. Not that it matters what I say; she doesn't give a solitary shit what I want.

'There, now,' she says, gripping my hands and pulling me to my feet.

My fingers are sore, and I wince and try to make her let go of my hands, but Eva-Lena turns around and puts them on her shoulders.

'OK, here we go.'

With her holding my palms firmly in place, I have no choice but to follow her through to the bathroom. For a split second, I tell myself that I could push her over, but I quickly realize that it's futile. She's so solidly built I wouldn't be able to move her an inch.

We get to the bathroom, and she parks me in front of the toilet.

'Trousers first,' she says, tugging them down with my underpants and then pushing me on to the lid.

The plastic is cool against my bare skin as she struggles with my tracksuit bottoms. My entire body is screaming no, but the less I want any of this, the more I tense up and can't manage to tell her that it's my damn decision whether to have a shower or not.

'Arms up,' she says, yanking my vest over my head. She pulls a face. 'This is going straight in the washing basket.'

It's chilly, sitting naked on the toilet lid and staring at Eva-Lena, and I get goosebumps. She turns on the water and moves a hand beneath the stream. Her plastic gloves are so tight they look like they could burst at any moment.

'You can come over now,' she says, holding her left hand out to me.

I briefly consider one last attempt to stand my ground, but when Eva-Lena raises an eyebrow I put my mitt in hers and get up, let her guide me over to the shower chair.

The water is too cold, but I can't be bothered to do anything but close my eyes. If I keep my mouth shut, this will all be over sooner. My thoughts turn to my old man and how it was always easier if I didn't make a sound. Rather than struggle, I follow Eva-Lena's orders, lifting my arms and holding my beard out of the way so that she can reach wherever she needs to. Nothing matters any more, after all. Sixten is gone.

A sense of emptiness spreads through me as Eva-Lena rinses me down. The more she scrubs with that ridiculous bloody sponge of hers, the redder my skin becomes, the more of me disappears.

By the time she closes the door behind her later, once I'm tucked back up in bed, I'm nothing but a shell. Emptiness echoes through me. *Don't want to go on, don't want to go on, don't want to go on.* That's the only thing going through my head.

# Thursday
# 3 August

MY MIND starts whirring the minute I stir and open my eyes. I haven't managed to get much sleep, but on the rare occasion I do manage to drift off, I keep replaying the moment when Hans got Sixten into his collar, dragging me back to reality and setting the nagging thoughts in motion again. I like to imagine myself arguing with our son, putting him in his place. Shoving him, even. Kicking him out of my house and telling him that this is where I draw the bloody line.

I glance down at my phone. He's ringing again, for the seventh time this morning. I snort and leave the damn thing to its shrieking.

Ingrid turns around. She looks like she is about to say something, but she changes her mind. Finishes wiping down the counter and then drapes the cloth over the tap. She makes her way over to the fire and adds another couple of logs. As she does so, her phone starts buzzing in her back pocket, and she fishes it out.

'I just need to take this,' she says, waving it in the air. 'I'll be back in a minute.'

I nod and hear her say her name before she closes the door behind her.

My phone starts howling again, but this time it's *Ellinor* that fills the screen. I pick it up and stare down at our bumblebee's name. I want to answer, would love to hear her voice. To ask what she's been up to today and how her summer job is going. To hear her share some memory of you, something we did when she was younger. But she's probably been talking to her dad. He'll have put her up to it, told her to give me a call.

I put the phone back on the nightstand and grunt. Reach for the spit cup and really put my back into it.

*8.10 a.m.*

*Bo feeling low, not in good spirits. Hans has called both the office and his father multiple times. Bo wants me to write that Hans isn't welcome here. Refusing to eat or shower. Left some chocolate by his bed and added a couple of logs to the fire.*

*Ingrid*

I WAKE and instinctively reach for Sixten, but he isn't there. The void reminds me of Mother, the way she always knew how to make the most difficult feelings disappear. The way she made life bearable.

I lower my head to the pillow and turn towards the kitchen. Blink and see my old man sitting right there in front of me. I'm at the other end of the table, trying to study my parents without them noticing. I've just finished the sandwich Mother made for me, and I glance over at her and take a sip of water. My old man has been quiet for several days now. I'm not the biggest fan of his chatter, but something about his silence makes me uneasy. As though he's trying to punish us, Mother and me.

'Lars-Erik . . .' she begins, putting a cautious hand on his arm. 'We'll be back on Monday, and I've left you plenty of food in the fridge.'

Mother's sister is getting married, and she and I are going to Hudiksvall together. Just the two of us, all weekend. I have the day off school on Monday in order to travel back. Aunt Karin is a few years younger than Mother, much taller and chattier. They used to have two brothers, too, but one of them drowned in the river when he was little, and the other popped his clogs in a car crash.

My father mutters something, and I turn to Mother again, worried that she might change her mind and decide to stay home. So far, she hasn't given in. I know she doesn't want to miss Aunt Karin's wedding.

'You can come with us, if you like . . .' she says, though she knows he would never do that. He isn't the least bit interested in her family.

'Pfft, what would I want to go to Hudiksvall for? I don't even know them,' he grunts, swigging from his bottle.

The look on Mother's face seems different somehow. There's a new sharpness to it, and I sense it isn't aimed at me. She turns to my father again, but he is still staring out of the window.

She gets up.

'Well, we'd better get going then. Can you carry the bag, Bo?' she asks, with such determination that I stand tall as I follow her out into the porch.

He is still sitting at the table, completely silent.

When we get to the main road, Mother starts walking so quickly that I struggle to keep up. The bag is heavy, and I have to bend my arm to stop it from dragging in the gravel. Her eyes are fixed ahead, but I keep glancing back over my shoulder. There is no sign of him, and the further down the hill we get, the more I finally dare to believe that we're actually going.

We have to catch a bus to Östersund, then a train to Sundsvall. From there, we'll get another train to Hudiksvall. I've only been on a train once before, to Ånge, but I was so young I don't even remember it.

Mother still hasn't said a word, and she doesn't slow down until we've passed the Johanssons' place.

'Are you OK with the bag, Bo? Is it heavy?' she asks anxiously. 'I was miles away.'

She takes it from me.

'It's OK,' I say, but I'm relieved all the same. My palms are stinging and red.

When we get to the bus stop, I stand so that I can see back up the hill, so she doesn't have to. Old Märtha shows up, and Mother seems cheerier than she did earlier. She tells her all about Aunt Karin's wedding, and I add that we're taking the train. Old Märtha laughs so hard I can see the gaps between her teeth.

Once we've boarded the bus, Mother's face cracks into a smile. She doesn't speak, just pats me on the thigh.

As the bus drives on to the ferry and the driver turns off the engine, she tugs at my arm.

'Come on, let's wait outside.'

The Vallsunda tragedy, when the ferry sank, had a real impact on her. It was years ago now, before I was even born, but she doesn't like taking the boat. Makes her jittery, she claims.

'There's no sense tempting fate,' she says, and I think she's right. She puts one hand on the rail where the only lifebuoy is hanging.

'I regret never learning to swim,' she says, looking down into the dark water.

I tuck my hand under her arm and remind her that I know how, if nothing else. That I was the first of all the kids to learn, over in the bay in Ranviken, where the water is shallow.

Mother smiles, and we gaze out across Storsjön, which is calm and flat. I wonder what the old man is up to at home. Whether he's still sitting at the kitchen table. Maybe he's out in the pigsty. Mother doesn't mention him; she almost never does. I glance over to her. We're having a good time, the two of us. Her eyes are fixed on Frösön, on the far side, and her thoughts are elsewhere.

I fiddle with the fabric of her skirt, then shove my hand into her pocket. After a while, her rough hand reaches down and squeezes mine.

I wake to what I think is someone knocking on the door, as I let go of Mother's hand and open my eyes. My gaze drifts across the floor, keen to see Sixten's reaction, but he isn't here. I close my eyes again, listening, but I can't hear anything. Must have imagined it, I think.

No, there it is again: a soft knocking, someone trying to open the front door. It always sticks, and you have to be really firm with it.

'Pull it harder,' the person says, just as the door swings open at last.

'Hello? Bo, are you home?'

'Come in,' I call in confusion, clearing my throat.

'It's us!' says the voice from the porch. It sounds like it belongs to a child. 'Aanta and Laara.'

Marita and Nejla's grandkids. Aanta's voice is familiar. They come over to sell lottery tickets sometimes. To fuss over Sixten and ask me questions.

'Stay. Sit,' Aanta says, and I hear the clicking of claws on the floor. Claws that need trimming. The absence of Sixten's weight by my side makes me want to cry.

'We brought Tjonne,' says Aanta, the oldest of the two boys, as he comes through to the kitchen.

I open my eyes. The dog is sniffing around the spot where Sixten used to lie.

'He can smell Sixten!' Laara chirps, running after him into the living room.

I can't quite read the look on Aanta's face, but there is something hesitant and pitying about it. He holds out a plastic tub.

'Here, Mum made you some soft gingerbread.'

I help myself to one of the biscuits.

'Oh, that was nice of her.'

After a moment or two, he takes a seat. Hesitantly pokes at the floor with his toes. Can only just reach.

I try to shuffle upright in bed.

'Hang on, I can make the bed tilt,' he says, getting back on to his feet. 'My *aajja* has one of these.'

Aanta grabs the remote control, and the head of the bed tilts upwards. I grin at his eagerness, but the empty feeling in my chest soon returns with a vengeance.

Tjonne comes running back through to the kitchen, his big body both supple and awkward somehow. He trots straight over to me and lowers his head to the edge of the mattress.

'I want a biscuit,' says Laara, sitting down on the floor in front of the fire.

'They're for Bo,' Aanta snaps at his little brother.

'But Mum said we could both have one when we got here.'

Tjonne lifts his head and goes to lie down beside Laara on the floor. He has left a damp spot on the sheets, just like Sixten after he's been at his water bowl.

'Of course you can both have a biscuit,' I say.

Aanta squints up at my face, trying to work out whether I'm being serious.

'Just take a plate from the washing-up rack, if you want one.' I nod to the sink.

Aanta hops down from his chair and goes to fetch a plate.

Laara runs his little hands across Tjonne's thick neck, right up to his ears. Sixten always loved being scratched there, too. Hans was also fond of dogs when he was little. Always sat close to the ones we had.

I feel a tug in my chest and struggle to come up with something to say. It's not like it'll make any difference. All I can think about is wanting Sixten up here with me. Stretched out beside my legs.

'We thought you might be sad,' Aanta says, putting his plate down on the bedside table. He opens the plastic tub and takes out two biscuits, passes one to his little brother. 'Because of Sixten.'

I'm powerless to stop the tears. It doesn't matter how hard I close my eyes, they still manage to seep out.

'I'd be sad too, if Tjonne had to go away,' he says.

Laara nods and leans against the dog.

We sit quietly. Aanta takes a bite of his biscuit and glances up at me. I use my hand to wipe my eyes, then take out my handkerchief and blow my nose. The sound makes Tjonne jump, and Laara bursts out laughing.

I point to the fire.

'You can add another log, Aanta,' I say.

'I want to, too!'

Laara leaps up from the floor and grabs a log of his own.

Watches what his older brother does, then follows his lead. Once that is done, he sits back down beside Tjonne and stares into the flames.

'Birch, of course,' I say, nibbling the soft gingerbread.

The two brothers nod, both absorbed by the fire.

Laara turns around and stares over at the biscuit box, but Aanta ignores him. His mind is elsewhere. He reminds me of you in that sense, the way you used to get lost in thought, some place far away.

'Have another,' I tell Laara, pointing to the plastic tub.

His little face lights up.

'Do you want one too?' he asks.

I shake my head and lean back against the pillow.

The boys stay a while longer, sitting in front of the fire. As they're leaving, Aanta turns around in the kitchen doorway.

'Mum says Sixten will be happy there,' he says, with such a serious look on his face that I can't do anything but believe him.

12.30 p.m.

*Bo still down, but in a slightly better mood than this morning. Tub of gingerbread on the table, doesn't remember who brought it. Fire OK. Heated some dill gratin for him, but Bo refuses to eat anything Hans has bought. I make some of his old favourite instead: rice pudding with lots of sugar, cinnamon and full-fat milk. A little goes down.*

*Ingrid*

# Thursday
# 17 August

I WAKE to a report on male contraceptive pills on the radio. The man has a thick Skåne accent, and he is talking about all the positive effects the medication has. Enabling him to sleep around without having to worry. Sparing his partners from all the horrible side effects women still have to endure on the regular pill.

Listening to him talk, I remember that you hated those pills. I thought you should just stop taking them, that there were other ways, but you insisted, said you wanted to make sure you didn't get pregnant again.

'I'm never coming back here,' you said firmly, when I picked up you and our newborn son from the maternity ward in Östersund.

I always wanted Hans to have siblings, would have loved a playmate of my own when I was a lad – though on the other hand, there was less risk of argument with just one. Hans never had to share with anyone. Micke from down by the church, his kids fell out so badly over their inheritance that they stopped speaking.

Ellinor never got any siblings either, and I wonder now whether that was intentional. It's not something Hans ever talked about.

'It's not the same, being a man today,' says the man from Skåne. 'There's a completely different set of prerequisites to becoming a father.'

I've never really thought about there being any particular prerequisites for that.

I stare up at the ceiling and wonder what Ellinor would make of all of this. Her relationship with Hans is so different from anything I've ever had with him. I remember her graduation from high school. She and Hans were both so forthright, somehow.

'I'm so proud of you,' Hans said, really emphasizing the 'so'.

He smiled, and she smiled back.

I had to look away, because it felt as if I was intruding. We were sitting in the shade of the birch in their courtyard, and your eyes welled up. I didn't know what to think.

Ellinor threw out her arms and hugged Hans, and I felt both embarrassed and proud.

I don't know why, but thinking back to that day irritates me. There's something about the way they're always hugging that I find annoying. Even if Ellinor is just going away for a day, she'll hug her parents. So many 'love you's back and forth.

My old man would never have said anything like that to me, and I've barely touched Hans since he was in primary school. It wasn't the done thing. Or was that just us, my old man and me? The thought of being in any way like him makes me grimace.

Looking back, you were also pretty touchy-feely with your family. With your father, siblings and mother. Hugging and carrying on to the extent that I felt uncomfortable.

The man on the radio doesn't seem to have any limits; he's now talking about erections and wetness. I don't understand half of what he's saying, but I'm still embarrassed. Why do people have to talk so much about everything nowadays?

Johanna changed the bedding earlier, and I run a hand over the fresh sheets. Fiddle with the corner of the beige duvet cover and try to remember the last time you and I made love. The physical side of things slowly ebbed away into something different. I remember thinking about it, but I never said anything. What could I have said? We could no longer do it the way we used to.

I don't even remember the last time I held you. Instead, the memories of you waving your arms and pushing me away have taken over. An embrace that quickly turned into a terrified look on your face.

'What are you doing?' you would shout, pushing me back.

As though I was a stranger who had hurt you. As though we hadn't been living together for almost sixty years.

'I miss it,' Ture said once, back when we were still able to go down to the park to watch people and eat ice cream. Every now and again, he would subtly nod in the direction of men he'd taken a fancy to. To show me, I assume.

I lower my hand to my crotch. Soft and lifeless. Nothing happens when I touch it these days, but that doesn't really bother me. I turn over in the hospital bed, on to my side. Cross my legs, then quickly roll on to the other side. My legs don't seem to know where to place themselves, and my left hand suddenly feels unnecessary.

It's always there, the Sixten-shaped hole. A nothingness that has amplified the emptiness you left behind. It's strange, but when Hans took Sixten I started missing you even more. Almost as though it was you he'd taken.

My ears strain for the sound of claws on the floor, for a soft yawn. For the sound of your knitting needles, gently clicking together. But all I can hear is the hum of the fridge and the ticking of the clock.

*5.15 p.m.*

*Bo in bed, hasn't touched his lunch. Re-heated it for him and made tea. Took out some chocolate. Doesn't seem to have much energy and still doesn't want to shower.*

*Ingrid*

I REFUSE to look at Hans. Fix my eyes on the cornicing and wait him out. What did he think? That everything would just go back to normal? That I'd forget all about his betrayal?

He's been coming over more often since he took Sixten. Filling the fridge and freezer with even more food, telling me that he's sorry every single time. I just ignore him, try to block out his stupid bloody mantra about doing it for my sake.

'Please, Dad. Are you planning to hate me for the rest of your life?' he asks, squeezing my upper arm.

I yank my arm back and make use of the only weapon I have left: my silence.

He sighs and gets up. Carries the bag of shopping over to the fridge and takes out yet another pack of jellied veal, even though I've barely made a start on the last one.

'I spoke to Ann-Katrin yesterday evening. Sixten is doing really well. She wanted you to know that they've been taking him on long walks every day,' he says as he closes the fridge.

I make a real effort to lie as still as I can. Tracing the line of the cornicing to the corner, then back again. Back and forth.

Hans sighs again.

'You're going to have to start talking to me at some point, you know.'

Back and forth, back and forth, lips tightly sealed.

'OK. I'll head off, then,' he says, lingering in the doorway.

But rather than leave, he comes back into the kitchen and

walks over to the fire. Adds one log, then another. I can't help but glance over at him. Haven't looked at him in days, possibly even weeks.

He is crouching down in front of the fire, using a log braced against the floor to keep his balance; his shirt has ridden up a little at the back. I open my mouth to say something, then decide against it. Can't quite swallow my anger.

Hans turns his head without warning, and I look up at the ceiling as quickly as I can. He sighs again, then gets up and heads towards the porch. His gaze bores into me, and I have to close my eyes to stop myself from looking at him.

'I'll be back at the weekend, probably on Saturday,' he says. 'It's Thursday today.'

He does up the zip on his jacket and reaches for the door handle. The moment he closes the door behind him, more quietly than usual, the tears start falling.

# Tuesday
## 22 August

I GLARE at the plate of food on the bedside table. The mash has started to harden around the edges.

Johanna spent a long time trying to convince me to eat it earlier, one trick after another. She said that me being stubborn won't bring Sixten back. That not eating isn't going to help. But what she doesn't understand is that refusing is all I can do.

I take a few sips of water from the glass she left. My hand is shaking, and the glass clinks as I set it down on the tray.

It doesn't matter what Johanna or anyone else says: I'm going to keep refusing, because I know it bothers Hans. I've seen all the ways he's been trying to make me forgive him, but I'm not going to bloody well give in.

Behind where I'm sitting in bed, the clock keeps ticking away. Without Sixten, the place feels deafeningly empty. All I can think about is the fact that he's not here.

A tractor drives by on the road, interrupting the ticking for a moment. My eyes drift over to the kitchen window. The August sunlight makes the dust shimmer, and I can't work out how I got into this situation. How could we have raised a son who would hurt me like this? One who makes everything so hard.

The sound of the engine fades into the distance, and the ticking returns. My stomach growls. I glance over at the worktop and see that there's a bit of coffee left in the machine. Get to my feet and immediately have to sit back down.

'I'll be damned,' I mumble before trying again. Stand still for a moment, waiting until the worst of the giddiness has passed.

The coffee is cold, so I pour it into the sink and head over to the fridge instead, eye up all the untouched meals from the past few days.

That's when I spot the tjälaknul Ingrid brought over. The slow-cooked elk meat has been cut into small pieces, mixed with plenty of brown sauce and spuds. My stomach rumbles.

'Had some left over from dinner yesterday,' she said a day or two ago, when she set the plate down in front of me.

I poked at it with my fork.

'And I can guarantee Hans didn't have a thing to do with it,' she said, as she poured me a glass of milk. 'Because I shot it myself.'

I put the plate into the microwave and find myself a fork.

As I wait, I gaze out through the window. Across the expanse of Storsjön, over towards Åreskutan. There isn't any snow on the mountain. Hans and Ellinor used to go skiing there when she was younger. I've only been a couple of times myself, always thought there was so much nonsense over there.

Right then, I see Tjonne running along the road. Aanta comes trudging along behind him, followed a moment or two later by Laara, who is carrying a stick in one hand.

They've been to visit a few times recently, but it isn't the same. Nothing can fill the void left by Sixten. If anything, it just makes it worse.

I shuffle closer to the kitchen window to check whether the boys are planning on turning off on to my drive, but they take a right down towards the swampy patch of land.

The microwave pings so loudly that I jump, and I have to sit down for a minute until my heart stops racing. Even heating up food leaves me short of breath nowadays.

Ingrid's leftovers go down a treat. The sauce reminds me of yours, maybe because she adds a bit of lingonberry jam the way you used to. I finish every last bite, then decide I'll do the washing up and drying, but my body feels so weak and heavy that I just dump everything into the sink for now. After that, I slump down on to my hospital bed and wipe my mouth. I actually do feel a bit better now.

But when I lower my head to the pillow, doubt rears its head again. Without warning, the anger is replaced by the clawing feeling in my chest. What have I done to deserve this? If you were here, maybe you would be able to explain. You always knew more about this sort of thing than me.

I reach for the jar containing your scarf. I don't even try to open it, just let it rest by my side where Sixten used to lie.

5.10 p.m.

*Bo asleep when I arrive. Lunch untouched. I try to tempt him with some frikadeller, but no luck. Not even interested in hot chocolate with cream. Also refused a shower.*

*Johanna*

# Tuesday
# 29 August

IT'S FIVE past ten when I call Ture. I'm careful not to do it too early, because he won't have had time to get his coffee ready.

I fiddle with the scrap of paper in front of me as I listen to the phone ring. A note to remind myself to ask him what he makes of young folks speaking English so much nowadays. I can't remember when I wrote it, but I thought it sounded interesting when I saw it this morning.

My eyes are drawn to the spot on the floor by the cabinets, the one where Sixten used to lie whenever he got too hot and needed to cool down.

The phone rings and rings, but Ture doesn't answer.

I hang up. Remember the exchange student Ellinor once brought home with her. He was from Canada, which meant I couldn't understand much of what he said, but Ellinor translated. I was so impressed; she sounded like an English professor.

I press the green button and *Ture* again, with the same result. Pushing the note away, I call him a third time. The shrill sound echoes down the line, but there is still no answer.

I decide to go to the toilet before I try one more time, staggering through the living room to the bathroom as thoughts of what might have happened torture me. All the places he could have fallen.

I tug down my tracksuit bottoms and underwear and slowly lower myself on to the seat. Stop being such an idiot, I tell myself. He's probably just spilled his coffee and needs to clean it up. That, or he forgot to take his almond tart out of the freezer. He'll have it in the microwave, which is why he didn't hear me ring.

I get back on to my feet and pull up my pants. Turn on the tap and hold my stiff fingers under the stream of water, wondering when Ture last washed his hands. I hold my own gaze in the mirror and try to shake off the worries. I never used to be like this, dwelling on things and getting myself all worked up, but every single part of my life is precarious now. I feel a sudden fondness for the old man in the mirror. It's not bloody easy, being human.

It's twenty past ten by the time I get back to the kitchen, and I flop down on to the bed, grab my phone and try again. Switch it to loudspeaker and lower the phone to the nightstand, listen to it ring.

The knot in my gut is getting bigger and bigger.

I press the red button and sit with the phone in my hand for a moment or two. I'll have to call Hans, I realize. Haven't spoken to him since the day he took Sixten.

My fingers start to shake, making it difficult to press the right buttons, and I accidentally end up in the directory rather than the list of recent calls. I go back. Hans has told me I just need to push the green button and then the down arrow until his name is in bold.

As it rings for what feels like an eternity, I have visions of Ture lying lifeless on the floor.

'Hi, Dad!' Hans sounds so happy that I lose my train of thought. 'Hello, are you there?'

'I'm here,' I say, heart racing. 'I can't get hold of Ture.'

We can talk about Sixten another time.

'What do you mean, isn't he answering the phone?'

'I've tried several times,' I say, my voice breaking. 'He usually picks up eventually.'

Hans covers the phone with his hand and says something in the background. That irritates me. How the hell did we manage to raise a son who can't recognize a serious situation when he sees one?

'Hello?' I snap.

'Sorry, I'm just in the middle of a meeting.' He sounds stressed now. 'Ture has carers too, right? If he's hurt himself, they'll be able to help. I'll try to get hold of him, though. I'll call you back as soon as I can.'

Hurt himself. That's true. It doesn't necessarily have to be the worst-case scenario. He could have just fallen and broken something. If that's what happened, I'll get Hans to drive me over to the hospital to visit him.

'Dad, is that OK?' Hans asks calmly.

'It's fine.'

He is quiet for a moment.

'I'm glad you called. Speak later.'

'OK,' I grunt. 'Thanks.'

I end the call before he has time to say anything else.

Despite the fact that I had to ring Hans, I feel less weighed down than I did before. More hopeful.

I get up to grab something to eat and decide that I'll take two whole packs of mazariner with me when I go to see Ture.

*12.54 p.m.*

*Butter-fried a bit of brown trout I brought with me. Bo worried about Ture, asks several times whether Hans has been in touch, but I haven't heard from him. Doesn't want to shower.*

*Ingrid*

HANS IS sitting on one of the dining chairs, a few metres away from me. He came straight over after work. He hasn't managed to get hold of Ture either, even though he called several times. In the end, he went over to his apartment and knocked on the door, but there was no answer. He eventually managed to get hold of one of Ture's carers, but they refused to tell him anything because he wasn't a relative, so now he's trying to speak to someone at the hospital.

Our son has the phone clamped to his ear as he waits, and his eyes are focused and bright. I'm so grateful that he's here right now.

Someone picks up, but I can't make out what they say. Hans frowns and explains why he is calling, but the person's answers don't seem to satisfy him.

He starts playing with his earlobe. We used to laugh at him whenever he read as a boy, because he would be so absorbed by the story that he was completely oblivious to us. Curled up on the sofa, one hand tugging on his ear.

I close my eyes and find myself praying. That they'll give us information even though we aren't blood relatives, Ture and me. That they'll tell us what happened.

My hand reaches for Sixten, desperate to feel his fur between my fingers.

I flinch when Hans raises his voice.

'Don't you understand what I'm saying? He doesn't have anyone other than my father, who is beside himself with worry.'

*Beside myself with worry.* I didn't think it was that obvious.

Hans nods and moves his phone over to the opposite ear.

'Yes, I'll wait,' he says, and I think I can see a slight smile.

I'm so proud to have such a capable and determined son, someone who is willing to make an effort for his father. If you were here, you'd be proud too.

But none of that matters, because the look on his face, when he says that he understands through clenched teeth, tells me that I'll never hear Ture's voice on the other end of the line again.

I can't stop them, the tears immediately start spilling down my cheeks, and I look up at Hans, as though it'll make any difference. As though he can help me.

I don't want to go on now.

'I'm sorry,' he says, putting a hand on my arm.

He really does look like he means it.

*8.35 p.m.*

*Hans called the office to say that Bo's friend Ture has passed away. Bo glum and quiet. Made tea with lots of sugar.*

*Johanna*

# Wednesday
# 6 September

*7.45 a.m.*

*Bo in bed, in and out of sleep. Low mood. Tells me to write that there's nothing to say when I ask how he is. Gave him medicine and left tea and porridge on table.*

*Ingrid*

I'M FLICKING through the local magazine Ingrid left on the bed-side table this morning. A picture of a boy, no more than ten years old, fills the centre spread. Blond curls frame his serious face, blue eyes staring straight down the camera. I reach for the magnifying glass. Without it, I can only read the headlines. The boy claims to have seen the Storsjö Beast, and he seems so proud in the picture, standing tall with a focused look on his face.

'Rubbish, of course it exists,' Ture said, the first time I told him that the whole thing was probably just a myth. 'How else do you explain people claiming to have seen it for hundreds of years?'

Until that point, I guess I'd thought he was joking whenever he pointed out a rogue wave in the middle of the lake, claiming that it was probably the beast coming up for air.

The boy in the magazine tells the reporter that he likes to go down to the shore at the weekend, and that sometimes he can tell the Beast has left marks on the beach overnight.

I quickly close the magazine. Don't want to remember, don't want to think about Ture. Don't want to think about the fact that I'll never again get to box him on the arm and say, 'Seen any monsters today, then?'

I grip the magazine in both hands and try to tear it in half, but the paper is too thick and my fingers too stiff. I try to toss it on to the floor instead, but it catches on the back of one of the chairs and is left hanging awkwardly.

1.10 p.m.

*Bo in a better mood. Says the priest came to see him. Sat down for a quick chat. Fish gratin for lunch. Reminded him to blow into bottle.*

*Kalle*

I LOOK up at the stocky woman in the chair. She's wearing the traditional black shirt and white dog collar. Her brown hair is tied up in a ponytail, and her glasses seem tight against her temples.

When I got down on to one knee in front of you, you asked whether I believed in God, and that made me nervous. I thought you might not want me if I was honest, but I couldn't lie, not if we were going to enter into a lifelong union together. So, keeping my face as straight as I could, I told you the truth.

'No, I don't, but I respect people who do.'

You studied me but didn't speak. Just sat quietly.

'I'll say yes anyway,' you said after several minutes, and I felt like I might burst. Couldn't stop grinning.

'I visited Fredrika last week,' the priest tells me. 'At Brunkulla-gården.'

I nod. It makes me happy to hear that, even though I know you probably wouldn't have recognized her. You were always fond of the priest. Said she did a lot for the youngsters in the parish.

'It's hard to watch someone you love go through that kind of change,' she continues.

I nod again, wonder whether anyone from her family has gone cuckoo.

It isn't the first time she's come to visit, the priest you saw several times a week for years. She dropped by before you left, and she's been back since. Still, it's been a while since she was last here.

I try to think of something to say, but I can't find the right words, so I look down at my hands instead. Talking about you is too hard. What is there to say? When the carers first started coming over, a couple of them insisted on asking and talking about you all the time. They said it must be tough on me that you were sick, and I never knew what to say but yes. It always created such an awkward atmosphere, and I just wanted them to go. To be left alone.

Despite all that, some part of me feels good that the priest is here today. That she went to the effort of going into town to buy a plant before coming over.

My mother was a churchgoer too, but not in any sort of forced way. To her, faith was as natural as the air we breathe, not something she ever gave much thought to.

I slowly twiddle my swollen thumbs and wonder why that sort of belief has always escaped me. Even when I was a boy, when I went to church with Mother. Because I did like it. During the winter, she would bundle me up in the kick-sled on Sunday mornings, and we would speed down towards the main road together. She always sat at the very back of the church, and let me drift off to sleep by her side.

I don't turn my nose up at religion the way Ture did, in other words. Maybe that's because you and Mother were both believers, active within the congregation, I think now as I sit here with the priest. But there is also something warm and human about the church. That was something we often talked about, but I don't think Ture ever really understood what I meant.

'They've got blood on their hands,' he snapped once, after I told him – with you in mind – that he'd made a mistake by leaving the church.

'Blood, eh?' I said. 'Surely they've done a lot of good too?'

He muttered something I didn't quite catch, and I couldn't work out why he was so angry about it. So dramatic.

I rarely joined you when you went to church, but I did go every once in a while. At Christmas and Easter. I'd put on the shirt you liked and slick back my hair. I used to enjoy watching you and the other women getting the coffee ready. You seemed as comfortable in the kitchen at the parish house as you did in our own.

I suppose I joined in when it suited me, and the same was probably true of my old man.

'Listen to your mother,' he always said, when she wanted to say an evening prayer with me.

He never said one himself.

The priest sips her coffee, and I find myself thinking that you and Mother were probably right. That you understood something I'd missed out on from the very beginning.

'How many years have you been married now?' she asks gently.

'Sixty-two years this spring,' I reply, and an image of you in your older sister's wedding dress fills my head. You were so much shorter than her that you had to take up the hem.

The priest raises an eyebrow and reaches for a piece of chocolate, pops it into her mouth. She pushes her glasses back on to the bridge of her nose and then wraps her hands around the coffee cup in her lap. She smiles, and I notice that she has dimples. I'd never realized that before. They suit her.

'I'm sure that doesn't make it any easier that she's sick,' she says in a serious voice.

I appreciate her honesty. She reminds me of Ingrid in that sense, in that she doesn't go in for much fluff.

I sip my tea, and the priest turns the plant she brought with her. You would probably be able to tell me the exact species, but to me it's just a red flower in a pot.

'I took one of these to Fredrika, too,' she says, nodding down at it. 'She seemed to like it.'

I give the priest a cautious smile. We sit quietly for a few minutes, but it feels good. The fire Ingrid lit this morning is still crackling away in the background.

We used to sit here like this together, you and me, getting lost

in the flames. We were similar in that regard. Never quite felt at
home if there wasn't a fire. There were days when a whole morning might pass without us noticing. We probably had the radio on,
and you were almost certainly busy making something.

'Time's strange, isn't it,' I say after a while.

She meets my eye but doesn't speak.

'Sometimes it moves so slowly, and then suddenly . . .' I move
my hand as fast as I can, demonstrating the way that twenty years
of my life just happened.

'That's the sort of thing we don't think about as children,' says
the priest. 'We just *were*, you know?'

I agree. One of my earliest memories is of my mother and I
pulling up beetroot together. I couldn't have been much older
than four or five, but I remember gripping the tops and yanking
as hard as I could, putting the beets on the pile with the others,
Mother telling me I was a good boy. And I was so proud.

'There comes a day when life on earth ends for all of us. That's
just how it is,' the priest says, helping herself to another piece of
chocolate.

I nod and glance over to the spot where Sixten's water bowl
used to be.

I wonder how he's doing now. Whether he has a sofa to sleep
on, whether they let him run off the lead. Whether he still bounds
about the way he used to in the meadow in the woods. I hope the
kids aren't bothering him too much.

I think about Sixten and I think about Hans. He's been on the
phone several times since we found out about Ture's death last
week, and I'm powerless to resist. It was as though something
inside me opened when I heard the news, and I haven't been able
to pull it back. Haven't been able to shut him out. To be angry
any more.

But the fact remains that he took Sixten. I can't forget that.

For a moment or two, I consider telling the priest. That my best
friend of five decades is dead, and that our son has taken away my

dog. But I don't know where to start. There's just so much about Ture that I want to get off my chest, and the whole Hans and Sixten business feels too complicated, too hard to explain.

The priest sucks on the piece of chocolate, and I wonder if I should tell her about Sixten after all. I take a deep breath, and am about to mention that I have an elkhound called Sixten when I change my mind and let out a deep sigh instead.

'It'll be OK, though,' she says, brushing a crumb from her thigh. 'In the end, it'll be OK. For all of us.'

That sounds a bit too simplistic, but when I meet her eye, something makes me believe her. She's probably right. Sixten might be getting hour-long walks now.

'Here, have some more chocolate.'

The priest pushes the plate towards me and takes another bit for herself.

I reach for a piece and murmur in reply. Place it on my tongue and leave it to melt.

I don't have the energy to talk any more.


Kalle puts a hand on my shoulder and gives it a gentle squeeze.

'Hello, Bo. How're we getting on today?'

I rub my eyes and say hello as he takes off his sweater and drapes it over the chair by the bed.

'You had visitors?' he asks, holding up the plant pot.

'The priest was here.'

Kalle pushes the chair back slightly so that he can swing his right foot up on to his left thigh. The wooden chair looks so fragile in contrast to his bulky frame.

We sit quietly for a moment or two, and I watch him as he holds the plant. His mind seems to be elsewhere. I like Kalle. He doesn't talk any more than he has to, and there's something pleasant about him. I've never heard him say a bad word about anyone.

At first, I probably thought it was a bit strange to have a bloke as a carer, but that doesn't bother me now.

'You know, my grams went to church with Fredrika,' Kalle says, lowering the pot to the table. 'I tagged along too, sometimes. When Mum was working.'

He gets up and goes over to the freezer to take out one of the ready meals. Pierces the film and puts it in the microwave. He is wearing a similar pair of tracksuit bottoms to the ones Hans bought me.

'I remember one of the old girls, the one who lived by the bay just after the eighty sign. She used to bake those biscuits with jam in, do you know the ones I mean?' Kalle asks as the microwave pings.

He carries the food over to the table and pours me a glass of milk. I know exactly which old woman and which biscuits he means. You used to bring a couple home for me.

'Grams let me eat as many as I wanted,' Kalle continues, chuckling so hard that his stomach jiggles.

I can't help but grin back.

# Saturday
# 16 September

HANS OPENS the door. I've been dressed and ready for at least half an hour now, sitting on a chair in the kitchen with my cane in my hand.

I should get up – I want to – but my legs are too weak, and they start shaking as I try to force myself out of the chair, even though I haven't used them much today. I feel a rush of anger at my body for failing me. Today, of all days, I want it to stand tall and carry Ture's memory. I look down at my legs, at my knobbly knees and the skinny thighs that have replaced my once-bulging muscles.

'Hi . . .' says Hans, knocking softly on the door frame.

I say hello and then point to a small badge in a box on the bed-side table.

'Could you help me with that?'

Hans takes out the little Storsjö Beast and studies the intricate details with a fond look on his face.

'Yes, this feels right today.'

He received his own fair share of Beast-themed birthday presents from Ture over the years.

Hans opens the clasp and carefully pushes the pin through the lapel on my jacket. The same jacket you helped me buy after my old man died. I thought it was needlessly expensive, but you said we should buy it for Mother's sake. And you were right, because she told me how handsome I looked three times during the funeral.

'Hang on, it's a little crooked,' says Hans, pulling the pin back out to straighten it up. 'There.'

His eyes look sad. I've been so preoccupied with myself that I forgot what Ture meant to him.

'Thank you,' I say, attempting a smile.

He hooks his arm through mine, and we walk out to the car together.

*10.15 a.m.*

*Taking Dad to Ture's funeral in Sundy. Wake in the church hall afterwards.*

*Hans*

HANS STARTS the engine and backs up towards the clear-felled area to turn around. He's driving slower than usual.

'What a beautiful day,' he says.

I follow his gaze out through the windscreen, across the golden-red landscape. Bydalsfjällen is wrapped in the mist that has crept up from Storsjön. This is your favourite time of year, but Ture always hated it when the autumn chill arrived. It made him wish he was a southerner, he said. He clung on to summer, walking around in his colourful shorts even when the cold came creeping in.

My eyes come to rest on the church tower down by the lake, where Ture is lying in a coffin. I try to imagine him dead, picture him as he looked when he dozed on the top bunk in the cabin.

If you were here, you would be sitting in the back seat, not saying a word about what you thought of Ture. That you didn't know what to do with his quirks.

There were times when I didn't either. Others when I was embarrassed, because he was odd in a way that sort of spilled over and made other people act strangely, too – but in a completely different way. They started to squirm, averting their eyes and turning away. That was why we spent most of our time together alone. Why we went up to the cabin.

But none of that matters now.

I look out at the hills and the lake again. I've been driving along these roads for nine decades, but I'm still struck by just how beautiful it is, and I never want to leave.

At the same time, I wish it could be the last time I ever see it as we pass the brow of the hill.


Hans indicates right and turns off on to the road to the church. It was a gravel track when I was younger, but these days the surface is smooth, and his electric car doesn't make a sound. There are spruces growing on our right, and I remember that we used to come down here together – Hans, Ture and I – to nick a couple at Christmas. Marita's parents had said we could take one from their property, but Ture preferred to steal from the church. I had to make Hans swear he wouldn't tell you, and I can't help but smile as I think about that now.

I gaze over at the trees beyond the church, where my mother and my old man are buried. I used to join her when she came down here on All Saints' Day, to plant the heather she'd brought with her. I think she picked something that would last a long time so she wouldn't have to come out here too often.

I remember glancing over at her during my old man's funeral. She was sitting with her head bowed and her hands clasped in her lap, and I thought she looked so small. Her grey hair was pulled tight at the temples; she'd twisted it into a bun at the nape of her neck, like always.

The church was almost full that day, and I turned around and let my eyes drift between the men from the sawmill in Ranviken. You were sitting by my side, and I was so proud. Let them wonder how the hell I'd managed to snare a girl as beautiful as you.

I was in my early thirties at the time, my father just over seventy when he died. They had me late in life, just like we did with Hans. We'd been together a few years by that point, but Hans still hadn't come along. I remember wondering if there was some sort of connection there, whether something in me and my old man made it difficult.

Mother was still looking down at her lap. Was there some part of her that was sad? Or was she relieved?

You were sitting with the hymn book in your hands, eyes closed, and I realized you were praying. That made something inside me soften, because I decided you were doing it for my sake and not my father's. You knew what things were like between us, yet I never heard you say a bad word about him, and I liked that. My anger was just that: mine.

The organist started playing, and Mother got up so suddenly that it made me jump. She walked forward to the coffin, and I moved over to her side. Seeing the picture of him there caused something inside me to shift. As though it was out of place, grating.

He had called me a few weeks earlier.

'Hello, it's me,' he'd said in his gruff voice.

'Hello,' I replied. I was surprised, because he'd never reached out on his own before, and I assumed something must be wrong with my mother.

'Uh . . .' he began.

'Has something happened to Mother?' I asked impatiently.

'What? No, there's nowt wrong with her.'

'OK,' I said, shifting my weight to the other leg.

'Uh, it was just . . .' His voice trailed off. He coughed and cleared his throat. 'Thought I'd see if you wanted to come over for dinner.'

I didn't know what to say, didn't understand what was happening.

'Right. When?'

'Don't know. Sunday?'

'I can't,' I blurted out. 'I've been invited to Fredrika's parents' place.'

'Ah,' he said. We were both quiet for a moment after that, but I could hear his heavy breathing down the line. 'Y'see, it was just . . .' Another pause. 'I could do with some help with the hound.'

Help with the hound. I couldn't exactly cancel the trip to see my parents-in-law just because he needed help with his dog.

'It'll have to wait,' I muttered, glancing over at the kitchen table. The flowers you'd put in a vase had started to wilt. 'It'll have to wait till another time.'

'Righto, s'pose it'll have to, then,' he said. We were both quiet again. It felt like he was about to say something else, that there was something weighing on him, but all I could hear was the sound of his breathing.

'Say hello to Mother for me,' I said after a moment.

'Ta-ra, then,' he said, hanging up.

I stood with the phone in my hand, staring down at the meadow buttercup in the vase. Its yellow petals had dropped to the table, and there was only one bud left on the stem. Maybe I should have just come out and asked what he really wanted, but as ever the words got caught in my throat and the anger took over.

It felt so false to stand there in front of his coffin. It felt so false that the mourners behind me thought I was grieving. The priest's words had annoyed me, respectful things that revealed he didn't have a clue who my father had been, and one part of me wanted to turn around and shout over the organ, to tell everyone that this man wasn't worth mourning. But I gritted my teeth and tried to swallow the lump in my throat. I stared straight into his eyes in the photograph, let my gaze drift over his clean-shaven chin, and got stuck there.

Mother tucked her delicate hand beneath my arm and dragged me back to the present. We took our seats, and the row behind us got up. I was so angry that I struggled to process people's nods as they passed us. They had no damn idea who I was, nor who my old man had been.

Beside me, Hans coughs. I've tried so hard to rid myself of my father, but he's still right there inside me, causing trouble. I take a deep breath. I'm not going to let him haunt me today, that's for sure. Today is all about Ture.

We pass the memorial grove where, a few days from now, someone will put up a small plaque saying *Ture Lindman*, and I remember all the times we played chess together in the park.

Hans slows down, and the big church building comes into view through the windscreen. Next time we're sitting together like this, Hans and I, it'll probably be for your funeral, and it occurs to me that you and I have never talked to him about where we want to be buried.

'I don't really want a headstone,' I say, gesturing to the graves from the last century. It's important he knows what we want.

'Dad . . .' Hans replies, as though my death is something distant and irrelevant.

I feel myself getting annoyed. Want to tell him that we've already decided to be laid to rest in Hissmofors and that I'll have a headstone after all – because you want one – but I don't speak.

Hans is quiet behind the wheel, slowly following the taxi up ahead. I wonder who could be in it. Someone from the chess club?

Our son seems tense. I think I see his right eyebrow twitch, the way it used to when he was on the verge of tears as a boy. That makes me feel stupid. I don't want him to think of me the way I thought of my old man. Don't want to be a thorn in his side.

'Your mum and I will have a headstone together,' I say, clearing my throat. 'It'll be just fine, you'll see.'

Hans pulls into the empty parking area and switches off the engine. He then turns to me and nods, and all I can see is you. That makes me feel calmer.

'Shall we go in?' he asks.

I WHISPER to Hans that I want to be able to see properly, so we walk to the front of the church. He asked me earlier whether I wanted to bring my walking frame, but I said no, I wanted to be able to walk up to the coffin with my head held high. He didn't argue, just nodded and opened the car door, helped me with my seatbelt.

On shaking legs, I sit down on the hard wooden pew. Ture would no doubt have had something cutting to say about the damn church. That they can't even give us decent seats.

The priest is sitting to the left of the lectern, clutching a stack of papers and a hymn book in one hand. Her eyes are fixed on the floor by her feet.

A large photograph of Ture as a young man has been propped up against the coffin, and he looks both familiar and like a stranger. It must be the same picture that hung on the wall in the office at the sawmill.

'Pff, madness,' Ture snorted, as we looked at the portraits that had been put up the day before. Management had decided that all the higher-ups would have their pictures framed. I just shrugged, couldn't understand why he was so annoyed.

I slowly turn around and spot Nisse and Sivert. They worked at the mill too, in the same job as Ture, but we never spent much time together.

Sivert raises his hand in a hesitant greeting and takes a seat on the other side of the aisle. Nisse has trouble sitting, and has to brace himself against the back of the pew in front. I wonder whether I seem as fragile to them.

A few rows further back, I see two women from Ture's building. He served on the tenants' committee for years. They're both smartly dressed, one of them wearing lipstick.

Malin, Ture's Ingrid, is here too, sitting in the middle of the big church. She's wearing a fleece with the home help logo on it, and I wonder if she has to get back to work afterwards. Either way, it was nice of her to come.

Organ music starts flooding from the speakers, and Hans passes me a rose. It's beautiful. Plump and blood red, exactly how I wanted it to be. I lower it to my lap and close my eyes, imagining you here beside me. You would have said something about the beautiful flowers, the music. You would have leaned in to me so that our shoulders touched and said that he was finally at peace.

I peer over at the coffin. Next time, it'll probably be your picture there, and a strange mixture of heaviness and anticipation settles over me. The thought of burying you feels surreal, absurd, but the idea of just getting it over and done with grows and grows. I'm ready to be done with everything now.

The music stops, and the priest starts talking. She repeats a lot of the things I told her over the phone, taking my words as her starting point, and for a moment it almost feels as though I'm the one talking up there.

The version of Ture's life she shares with us sounds a bit like a fairy tale. She starts in Hissmofors, explaining that his parents expected him to study elsewhere before coming back. That his father had studied in Gothenburg, too. Her voice is powerful, so different from what it was like during our chat in my kitchen recently, making it sound as if she knew him, too. As if she's proud of him, which makes me feel calm.

I follow her subtle hand movements and find myself thinking that it would be nice if she conducted your ceremony when the time comes. That, even though your funeral will be in Hissmo-fors, she might be willing to make the journey over for the day.

The priest says that Hissmofors was too small for Ture back then, that he needed something different, something more, and I wonder who could have told her that. Because that isn't the way I described it.

She looks out at the scattered group of people in front of her and is quiet for a moment. I get the sense that her eyes are on someone sitting at the very back of the church, but I can't see who it is when I turn my head.

'Gothenburg was that something, and he got to experience a new kind of life there,' she continues. I wonder what she means by that. It sounds a little hazy.

For a moment, I imagine what it would be like if I were the one up at the microphone, but no one thought to ask. The people in my life don't count on me any more, and they're right not to, because my body isn't up to it.

'The Ture we knew wasn't afraid of living,' she says.

Those were my exact words: that the Ture I knew wasn't afraid of living. That he had travelled all over the world.

I remember him coming back from a trip to Tunisia after an entire month away. That felt like such a long time, and I had started to miss him. He brought all sorts of things back with him, told me about the food he'd eaten and the people he'd met. He seemed so lyrical and spirited.

The priest clears her throat and turns over the sheet of paper in her hands. A sudden weariness hits me, and I close my eyes. I think about what I'd like the priest to say about you. What Hans will say, because he'll no doubt want to give his own speech. Ellinor might, too.

'Ture lived a long life,' says the priest.

That's why the church is so empty. Almost everyone he knew is already dead.

In the end, his heart gave out. That was what the hospital staff

told Hans. I wonder whether he was calm or whether he pan-
icked in those final seconds. I imagine him laid out in bed with his
clothes on when they found him, and the thought that he might
have felt lonely makes my stomach turn. That I wasn't there. That
the only person who really cared about him wasn't there.

The priest stops talking, and the organist starts playing again.
My chest feels tight, and I squeeze my eyes shut. I don't know
why, but I don't want anyone to see my tears.

Right then, I feel a weight on my right thigh. Through blurry
eyes, I see Hans's hand on my leg. Resting there the way my hand
used to rest on his shoulder after we'd spent a little too long out
fishing in clothes that weren't quite warm enough. I'm struck by
how alike they are, our hands. How old his hand looks.

I put mine on top of his.


On our way out, I get a better look at the man sitting in the back
row, the one the priest's eyes seemed to linger on earlier. He's a
few years younger than me. Well dressed, in an expensive-looking
jacket and tie, with a big black hat on the pew beside him. As I
pass, I notice that he's holding an envelope. I slow down and think
I can make out the word *Ture* written in looping letters.

Once we're out of his eyeline, I gently tug on Hans's arm. I nod
towards the display board full of information about the church,
and Hans leads me over. I turn to look at the stranger. He is still
sitting in the back row, still in the same position.

The priest walks slowly down the aisle after the mourners, but
when she spots the man she turns off into the row in front of him.
Holds out a hand and says hello. He returns the gesture in a way
that tells me they've spoken before. They exchange a few words I
don't catch, then she nods and continues on her way.

'We'll be right there,' I tell the priest as she passes.

'Take your time,' she says, and Hans flashes her a quick smile.

The man gets to his feet at long last. He picks up his hat and makes his way over to the coffin. Pauses in front of the photograph and holds the hat to his stomach with his eyes closed.

I feel a tingling sensation in my legs.

'Who is that?' asks Hans.

I shrug. 'No idea, never seen the bloke before.'

The man is still standing with his eyes shut. Maybe he's praying or talking to himself. The curiosity almost makes me feel annoyed.

'Fancy clothes,' Hans mumbles.

He definitely stands out. I'm sure I've never met him before, because I would remember someone who looked like that.

The man opens his eyes and looks down at the envelope in his hand. He hesitates for a moment, places it on top of the coffin, then quickly turns around and starts making his way out.

'We'll have to ask,' says Hans.

Before I have time to speak, to tell him that we can't, he has taken a step towards him.

'Hi, I'm Hans, and this is my dad, Bo. He was a close friend of Ture's.'

The man pauses, but doesn't speak. Just nods solemnly. I can't manage a single word.

'How did you know Ture?' Hans asks after a moment.

'We . . .' The man trails off.

I might be imagining it, but it feels as though he is studying me from head to toe.

'We were acquaintances in Gothenburg.'

He clears his throat and puts on his hat. I've only ever seen people wearing hats like that on TV.

'My dad and Ture worked together at the sawmill in Hissmofors,' Hans continues. 'Right, Dad?'

'We did,' I say, finding my tongue at last.

I hold out a hand.

'Bo.'

The man takes my hand in a firm grip.

'Eskil.'

Eskil. Ture never mentioned anyone called Eskil.

We stand quietly, the man stroking his neat beard. I'm struck by how clean he is. The kind of person who makes you feel filthy, even though you aren't.

'So you're from Gothenburg?' Hans asks, and yet again I'm glad he's here with me.

Eskil clears his throat. I can't put my finger on it, but there is something about him that really irritates me.

'Yes, I am. From Gothenburg.'

Hans says that he's been there quite a lot with work, that it's a great city, and the man nods.

'Are you staying for coffee in the hall?' Hans asks.

Eskil shakes his head. 'I have a plane to catch, so I'm afraid I can't,' he says, straightening his jacket. 'But it was great to meet you both. Goodbye.'

And with that, he hurries out of the church. I'm not sure whether I'm relieved or disappointed.

'Shall we head over to the hall, then?' Hans asks, holding out his arm.

I take it, and we make our way out. With my eyes on the golden yellow birches down by the lake, I wonder why Ture never mentioned this Eskil bloke. They must have been pretty close for him to go to the effort of flying up here from Gothenburg. I suppose it was because he didn't want to, and I feel a sudden glumness at the thought that there were things Ture chose not to tell me.

The air is crisp and cool, and I fill my lungs as we pause on the steps outside. Watch the man getting into a taxi.

'He was a bit weird, huh?' says Hans. 'Why wouldn't he say who he was?'

I shrug. I have my suspicions about how Ture knew the man, but I don't know how to explain that to Hans. We've never talked about why Ture never married or any of that business. Hans takes a step down, and I follow him. It's windy, and my beard stirs in the breeze. The Swedish Church flag by the entrance flaps slowly, and I wonder whether there are things you've never told me. Whether there are things you've never told anyone. But then I remember how you and your little sister could be. You were only a year or so apart, and people thought you acted like twins. Giggling at things that didn't seem funny to me.

My eyes come to rest on a row of canoes lined up by the shore.

No, you probably told her everything.

Hans pauses and gazes over at the trees beyond the canoes. The red aspen leaves tremble in the wind. I wonder whether he has secrets, too.

'The girls in my class used to run down there to pick cowslips for our teacher at the end of term,' he says, his eyes on the lake. 'I thought they were so pretty, so I joined them one year, picked a bouquet of my own. Do you remember what happened then?'

I shake my head. 'No?'

'Gunnar squirted water all over my shirt just as we were about to go into the church. He called me a girl, and I burst into tears and ran over to you and Mum,' he says. 'And then I sneaked out to find some leeches from the bay. I put them in the pocket of his coat, because he'd left it in the hall. Don't you remember?'

Hans leans forward, unable to stop the laughter. His big body sways, and I can't help but join in.

'God, that caused such a fuss,' he says, drying his eyes.

'I bet,' I say, as my laughter gives way to a coughing fit.

'He started it, though. Gunnar was such a shit,' Hans says, thumping me on the back.


The tables in the church hall have been laid with white cups and floral serviettes, and we drink coffee and eat mazariner. The priest grabs a cup and sits down with us.

'Ahh, a spot of fika is just the ticket,' she says.

I try to forget all about the man in the hat and scan the room for Malin instead. Want to say something to her, not that I know what. Just so she knows how important she was to Ture. But I can't see her anywhere. She probably had to get back to work, as I suspected. I start picking at my almond tart in its foil tray.

The coffee is delicious, and I ask Hans to fetch me another cup. Sivert and Nisse get up from one of the other tables and make their way over.

'Hello, Bosse,' says Sivert, holding out a hand.

We chat for a while, mostly about the summer. It's been unusually warm, they say, and I make it sound as if I agree, though I can't remember thinking the heat was anything special. Nisse tells me that he spent a few weeks looking after his daughter's dog, that it was unusually lazy because of the high temperatures. I study his face, his neat moustache, and realize that I haven't thought about Sixten all day. Get upset at the thought that he isn't back home, waiting for me.

Sivert and Nisse have turned their attention to Hans, who is telling them about his job. They both seem genuinely interested.

I start thinking about the man in the hat again, and I decide that my suspicions are probably correct, that he was someone Ture was involved with. I stroke my beard. Look down at my hands and ask myself again why Ture never mentioned him. My nails are nice and neat, because Ingrid helped me trim them the other day.

I run a thumb along my swollen index finger. Ture's romantic life always felt too private. It wasn't as though we spent all that much time talking about you either, but when I saw the mysterious man in the church earlier, it was like something happened to me. I felt offended somehow. It dawned on me that there were parts of Ture I had no idea about, despite the fact that I was his best friend.

A squeaking sound by the door makes me look up. The caretaker is busy unfolding a ladder by the accessible toilet, and he climbs to the top to reach the light bulb on the ceiling. I'm impressed by his balance. It's been a long time since I could do something like that.

I regret not asking Ture more when I had the chance. What he got up to in Gothenburg, for example. I study Hans, Sivert and Nisse, and hope he didn't think I had no interest in finding out more about him.

Without warning, I feel so tired I could nod off. Can't keep my eyes open. Hans tells Sivert that he's taken the day off, and I wonder how many days he'll take off when I die.

Right then, I feel a hand on my back.

'Suppose we should make a move,' says Hans.

'Yes, it's probably time to round things up here soon, anyway,' says the priest, glancing down at her watch. 'I have to pick up the kids.'

I nod at the priest, who smiles.

'Did you doze off there?'

Hans tells me to wait by the door while he brings the car over, and I don't argue. Other than Sivert and Nisse, we're the last people here. I lift a hand to my mouth and yawn, don't know how I'm going to stay awake until we get home.

# Monday
# 25 September

*8.10 a.m.*

*Bo asleep when I arrive. Woke him and made porridge, but he soon dozed off again. Seems increasingly tired. Left a sandwich by his bed.*

*Johanna*

I WAKE up shivering. Turn my head and see a dry open sandwich on the bedside table. I need to pee, but just the thought of getting up to go to the toilet leaves me exhausted. I can barely lift my legs and my head is heavy on the pillow, so I reach beneath the covers and feel my crotch. Sure enough, they've got me in a nappy. The hot urine feels good at first, but once my bladder is empty the feeling transforms into shame.

Do you feel ashamed when this sort of thing happens, or are you beyond all that?

I reach for your scarf jar and awkwardly try to open the lid, but in vain. Let it drop down on to the mattress beside me.

*12.20 p.m.*

*Bo in bed. Nappy full. Heated some fish balls. He ate a little. Chatted about Fredrika and mushrooms. Says he's tired and doesn't have any appetite. Left water and chocolate by his bed.*

*Ingrid*

THE FIRST thing I notice when I wake is your scent. I turn my head and feel your soft scarf against my cheek. Take a deep breath and drift off again.

# Tuesday–Friday
# 10–13 October

I CAN hear Ingrid's voice, but it's hard to make out what she is saying. She's reading aloud from a book, I think, as I slowly force my eyes open. The bright light makes them sting. Ingrid is sitting in a chair by the bed, a picture of a wolf howling at the moon on her T-shirt. I'm cold.

She pushes her glasses down on to the tip of her nose.

'Hello there,' she says, lowering her book to the nightstand. 'Are you thirsty?'

I nod. My tongue is dry.

She gets up and walks over to the kitchen, returns with a damp cloth.

'Do you want a bite to eat, too?' she asks, dabbing the cloth on my lips. 'We can try some of this strawberry drink.'

I close my eyes and listen as she unwraps the straw on the bottle of nutritional supplement. The soft plastic rustles as she tells me about the bright colours in the forest, that the leaves look like they're ablaze at the moment. Her voice ebbs away, and I see you wandering among the flowers on the other side of the road. Moving in and out of my field of vision, in a body that spans your entire lifetime. You drift through the shadows of the pines and change shape, over and over again. Young, pregnant, confused.

Right then, I notice Ingrid and Sixten walking towards me. He's off the lead, striding along like a competition dog. Running around the way he always does when he's got the zoomies. Up ahead, towards the bend by Evertsson's place, I see my old man coming towards me with a spade. Mother is a few metres behind him, trudging along with a stooped back and her arms resting behind her against the base of her spine. Sixten speeds up, bolting down the slope to greet them.

I feel a tug in my chest, and it gets harder to breathe. My throat tightens. I try to open my eyes, but can't.

'Are you OK, Bo?'

I manage to get them open and feel a little better when I see Ingrid's face. She's frowning.

'Is it uncomfortable?'

I don't really know what she's talking about, but I nod anyway. I do feel a kind of uncomfortable sensation. Ingrid sits down on the edge of the mattress and puts a hand on top of mine. Her palm is warm and slightly clammy.

'Everything will be OK soon,' she says, and I cling to her words.

Someone knocks on the door, and I hope it's Hans. I want him here, to look him in the eye and say that I only want the best for him. That, despite my stubbornness, I'm proud of him. I just want him to know.

It's something I've been thinking about since we met that Eskil bloke at Ture's funeral, that I don't want to leave anything unsaid. That I don't want it to be like it was with my old man.

For some strange reason, I'm not angry any more. Hans was only doing what he thought best, and Sixten is probably happy in his new home.

The door opens.

'That must be Sofia, the new temp,' says Ingrid, getting to her feet. 'You met her last week.'

I nod, though I don't remember. I'm just glad it isn't the battle-axe. Ingrid disappears into the porch, and I wonder when Hans will be here. I'm too tired to turn my head, so I rest my eyes once she is gone. Give myself over to sleep again.

Hans hurls himself down on to the ice. Stretches his legs and lets his skates hit the frozen water, leaving small nicks on the surface. He lies perfectly still, staring up at the sky for a moment. You get up from the kick-sled.

'Mind you don't get a cold bum,' you say, making your way out on to the sheet of ice. It can't be much more than twenty metres wide, a frozen pool in the middle of the meadow in the woods.

He never got tired of skating, wanted to go down there every single day that winter. I didn't either. But just one year later, it was too small for him. He wanted to go down to the rink by the school with Isaksson's boys instead.

'Hi, Bo,' says a girl's voice, and I see a young, unfamiliar face looming over me. The girl can't have finished school, I think. Can't be much older than fifteen.

I try to open my mouth to say hello, but it doesn't work.

'Sofia is here to help me get you washed,' Ingrid explains, placing a hand on my leg. 'We're going to change your nappy.'

The temp ties a plastic apron around her waist and pulls on a pair of gloves. Ingrid stamps on the pedal to release the brakes, then pulls the bed out a little so the girl can squeeze around the other side.

'Your way or mine?' the temp asks.

'Up to you. It doesn't matter to me.'

I look up at Ingrid and the temp, who are standing on either side of me, and wonder what you're doing right now. Whether you're feeling agitated or calm.

'OK, we're going to get you to roll on to your side in Sofia's direction,' Ingrid says, as the temp grips my right arm and pulls me towards her. A moment later, I'm lying on my left-hand side.

Ingrid tucks a plastic sheet beneath my backside, and the temp lowers me down on to my back. It all happens so quickly that I barely have time to think.

'And now we need you to come this way,' says Ingrid, taking my left arm and pulling as the temp smooths out the plastic sheet on the other side. 'There, now. That'll help keep your bed nice and clean.'

Ingrid pushes my flannel shirt up and tugs at the waistband on my tracksuit bottoms, as though to check that the elastic works. She then pulls them down at one side.

'We're going to get you into a fresh nappy now,' she says. 'I'll do it.'

The temp gives her a cautious nod in reply.

'Come this way again,' she says, taking my right hand and pulling. I try to resist, it's always easiest that way, but my muscles don't respond the way I want them to.

Ingrid wipes my backside with the warm cloths. It feels good.

They then roll me on to my back again. Ingrid straightens my trousers and shirt, and pulls the blanket up over me.

I can feel the familiar tugging sensation in my chest, but I don't know what to do about it. Breathing gets harder again.

'That was nice, wasn't it, Bo,' says the young girl, putting a hand on my upper arm. I look up at her, and she smiles and turns away.

I glance at Ingrid then, and she meets my gaze. I cling to her blue eyes and feel myself calm down. We sit like that for a while, and she nods. No one speaks. I don't want to, want to stay right here with her, but then I start dozing off.


I wake to the sound of Ingrid's voice.

'Here,' she says, passing her work phone to the temp. 'Can you call the priest?'

The girl takes the phone and raises an eyebrow.

'OK . . . but is he even a Christian?'

Ingrid, who is hunched over the bag of things from the office, stops whatever she is doing. Looks up at the temp with a pack of gloves in one hand, and thinks for a moment. She then turns to me.

'I wouldn't say you're a Christian, are you? Not that it really matters,' she says with a smile. 'I think Bo likes talking to the priest anyway. Plenty of people do.'

I linger on Ingrid's face and realize that what she just said is true. That it's done me good to talk to the priest in the past. That, when it really comes down to it, we just don't know.

I'm lying here, about to die, and I just don't know.

My thoughts turn to Ture, to when he died. What went through his head in that moment? What will you be thinking about when your time comes?

The temp follows Ingrid's eyes and looks down at me, too. She seems confused.

Without warning, a laugh bubbles up inside me and all sorts of strange sounds seep out.

Ingrid presses a hand to her mouth and joins in. The temp's eyes widen, and then, hesitantly, she starts laughing too.


The smell of coffee brings me round, and Ellinor greets me with a smile.

'I love you!' she blurts out. 'And so does Dad,' she adds, before I have time to blink.

I look up at our bumblebee and am flooded with emotion. Over by the kitchen counter, Hans laughs, but he sounds troubled. Probably tugging on his earlobe, I think. I want him to come closer so I can see him properly.

It's incredible that our Ellinor is so big, absurd that time could have passed so quickly. Lying here in bed, it's hard to comprehend.

'He's getting the fika ready. We've got almond tarts,' Ellinor explains, stroking the back of my hand.

I try to smile. I don't know whether it works or not, but Ellinor tucks her hand beneath mine so that I can stroke it with my thumb.

My thoughts turn to mazariner, to Ture. I don't really believe it, but I hope we'll see each other soon. That he'll meet me somewhere. Somewhere I'll eventually see you again, too.

An image of Ture standing by the wood burner in the cabin

comes back to me. I remember how much of an effort he made to make Hans feel comfortable whenever we went up there to fish. How he always bought the biscuits Hans liked.

Hans comes over with the coffee and almond tarts, and he sits down beside Ellinor. He smiles at me and I feel an urge to say that I'm proud of him, that I did the best I could, but they're talking about Ellinor's studies, about what sort of job she might apply for once she's finished, and I don't want to interrupt.

'I'll probably start with social services,' she says. 'That's what most people do.'

'Sounds smart. A secure job, right, Dad?'

I smile. He knows what his old man thinks, and that makes me proud.

'Working with people, that'll be perfect for you,' he says, putting a hand on our bumblebee's head.

'Perfect,' I mumble.


My mouth feels so dry, like it might crack. I press my lips together and try to moisten them, but it doesn't help.

'Here's Ingrid with some water,' says the priest.

I open my eyes and see Ingrid coming towards me. The priest is sitting by my bed.

'I think we should try a little ice cream,' says Ingrid.

I give her a cautious nod.

'Ice cream it is,' says the priest.

Ture and I used to buy ice cream in the park during the summer, and the cold cream feels as good in my mouth now as it did then. The priest says something I don't catch, then gets up and grabs a blanket from the armchair in the corner, drapes it over my feet. That's nice, because they do feel a bit icy.

I wonder whether she has been to see you lately, and I want to ask about you, whether she thinks I'm still inside you somewhere. Whether she thinks we'll be together again one day. But then the shortness of breath hits me, making it difficult to fill my lungs properly.

I part my lips and try to say your name, but the tiredness overwhelms me.


'I'll put this here. Can you feel it on your cheek?' Ingrid asks, as your scent hits my nose.

She adjusts the scarf, fluffing it up around my throat and cheek. The room disappears. All that exists is the soft fabric and your scent.

I put everything into it and take a deep breath. Hold the air in my lungs until it forces itself out and I drift off again.


The next time I wake, Mother is in my thoughts.

Ingrid dabs my lips, and I feel a cool breeze on my face.

'I thought I'd open the window. A bit of autumn air is nice, isn't it?' she says, dipping the cloth into the bowl of water.

I nod. My mother taught me all the important things in life. About dogs and animals, things I couldn't have lived without.

They said she died quickly. When the staff went in to wake her one morning, she was already gone. Lying flat on her back with her mouth and eyes open. Hands clasped on top of the covers, they said, as though she'd planned it that way.

I gasp for air, feel the tightness again. Don't really want to think about it, because it hit me hard when Mother died. I remember you saying that you knew how upset I was. I grunted something in reply, but I never told you the truth: that I was sad for months afterwards. That I missed her terribly.

I regret never thanking her for being her. For being so much better than my old man. I should have told her that, but I never did. I realize now that I let my anger towards him get in between us, and that meant I could never truly be happy when we spent time together.

I'm breathless and afraid, can't quite manage to open my eyes. Maybe this is it, I think. Maybe this is how it feels to die. A force pulling me deeper and further away.

But then Hans puts a hand on my forehead, and breathing suddenly feels easier again. The same way I put a hand on his when he had pneumonia. He was off school for a full month.

He lets his hand rest there, and I can tell that there is nowhere else he would rather be.


I wake feeling queasy, like I've eaten something bad, but I don't remember when or what I last ate.

'Is it normal for it to take this long?' Hans whispers.

Am I not dying fast enough? I feel like a burden. Like I'm stopping Hans and everyone else from getting on with all the other things they need to do.

I open my eyes and meet our son's. At first, he looks so unhappy, but when I nod, his face cracks into a smile.

'He's awake.'

'Mmm,' I mumble, which makes him laugh.

Ingrid sets down a bowl of water on the bedside table and smiles at us.

Just like that, I feel much brighter. Looking up at our son, my old man comes back to me. There are parts of him that Hans and I both share. His jaw, for example. All three of us have that.

Our son is here, at the very least. Sitting by my side.

I wasn't by my father's side when he died.

It took him a long time to go. Several days. He was in hospital, full of tubes and on medication for the pain. Mother stayed by his bedside, dabbing his forehead and reading to him from the local paper.

I stopped by a few times, for her sake, so she wouldn't feel alone. Though I also didn't want him to get any ideas.

He looked so small and pathetic as I stood there by his bed, and I felt the familiar grating inside. I remembered his phone call from a few weeks earlier, and some small part of me wanted to put a hand on his shoulder.

After everything that happened with Buster, and the older I got, the more I realized I had nothing to gain from that man. I switched him off inside me. Turned my back on him and built a life of my own, as I wanted it to be.

Despite all that, it never disappeared entirely, that desire to have him look at me. A look that said: good job, Bo.

When I got to the hospital, it had been so long since I last felt any warmth towards him that I couldn't even remember when I ever had. So when Mother called to say that the doctors had said he had only hours left, to ask if I wanted to come to the hospital, I said no. That I had to work. It was a Monday, after all.

And yet, when she called again that evening to say that he was dead, something inside me broke.

Hans shifts in his chair beside the bed. His hair is getting long, hanging down over his forehead. He doesn't seem to have any of that sticky stuff in it, because it looks soft and fluffy, the way it did when he was a boy. I feel an urge to ruffle it, but don't have the energy to lift my arm.

I realize now that I never really knew my old man, not the way I know Hans. Despite all our squabbles, we belong together in a way my father and I never did.

I look up at Hans and don't want him to feel like something inside him has broken when I'm gone. Don't want it to eat away at him for decades.

I know what I want to say, but it's hard. I've been trying to say it for weeks now. They're just words, but it's so hard.

'You know . . .' I whisper, gasping for air.

He nods slowly. Raises one eyebrow and smiles softly, to let me know that he's listening.

Looking at him, all I see is you. I take another breath. It's hard to fill my lungs, and I really have to fight the tiredness.

'You know I'm proud of you,' I eventually manage to whisper. 'And your mum is too.'

Hans gazes at me with a look I'd forgotten, the same look he used to give me as a boy. When his eyes lit up at everything I said, letting me know that we were a team.

He blinks.

He then leans forward and kisses me on the forehead.

'I know, Dad.'

I hear the clicking of claws and smell his familiar scent before my palm even registers his soft fur.

'Do you really think he knows?' Hans asks.

'I'm sure of it,' says Ingrid.

My body rocks as Sixten jumps up into his usual spot beside my left leg.

A sense of calm spreads through me. He realizes that I can't pat him with my hand, so he lowers his head to my stomach.

'Are you going to be OK?' Hans asks. 'With Sixten and everything, I mean.'

'We're fine, Hans. We'll be just fine. Bo, Sixten and me.'

I feel something on my right shoulder, and it takes me a moment to realize that it's Hans's hand. He squeezes it tightly, holds it for several minutes. He might have said something too, but I can't hear.

None of that matters now, because everything feels right.

'Bo has nothing to worry about. Everything is as it should be, and it's all going to be OK,' Ingrid tells him, and I believe her.

Hans's hand is still on my shoulder, and I imagine reaching up and putting mine on top of it. Telling him that I did my best, that I hope he knows that. The heat of his palm spreads through the rest of my body, and I no longer feel cold.

The door swings shut.

Ingrid takes my left hand and lowers it to Sixten's back. Her skin is so warm.

I see Sixten's powerful body running up ahead of me, charging into the meadow in the woods at full pelt. He comes racing back towards me before turning off towards the stream to cool down.

Everything is just as it should be, I think, right before I doze off.


It's dark, and I can't see a thing, but the scent of Sixten's coat finds its way in, causing something inside me to shift. To be rearranged. I feel his damp nose digging beneath my palm, and he presses himself against my body. Everything is crystal clear.

A window opens, and I hear the cranes gathering to fly south.

*3.30 a.m.*

*Bo passes away quietly in his sleep. He looks so peaceful, not in any pain. His hand was on Sixten, who is lying by his side. I've lit a candle and called Hans.*

*Ingrid*

# Discussion questions – *When the Cranes Fly South*

- The inspiration for *When the Cranes Fly South* first came about when Lisa Ridzén found notes left by the home care team that was looking after her grandfather during his final stage in life, to keep her family in the loop on his days and his condition. In what way do you feel the home care team's notes about Bo serve the novel's narrative?

- Author Lisa Ridzén has conducted research on masculinity norms in rural communities. Do you feel that is evident in this novel? In what ways?

- Bo is very set on having Sixten remain with him, whilst his son Hans claims it would be better for everyone if Sixten were to stay with someone who's better able to take care of him. Do you see where both perspectives are coming from, or did you take sides as you were reading?

- A central theme in the novel is father-son relationships; Bo's relationship with his own father and the relationship between Bo and his son Hans. Which of these portrayals affected you the most, and in what ways did the novel make you reflect on your own close relationships?

- Bo's wife Fredrika is constantly present in the novel, even if she no longer lives with Bo. How do you perceive Bo and Fredrika's relationship and what did you think of the narrational device in having Bo address Fredrika in the novel?

- How much did you know about life and culture in Sweden, especially the far north, and did you learn anything new?

On a station platform, with nothing to read,
and a four-hour train journey stretching ahead of him...

That's where the story began for Penguin founder Allen Lane.
With only 'shabby reprints of shoddy novels' on offer,
he resolved to make better books for readers everywhere.

By the time his train pulled into London, the idea was formed.
He would bring the best writing, in stylish and affordable
formats, to everyone. His books would be sold in bookstores,
stationers and tobacconists, for no more than the price
of a ten-pack of cigarettes.

And on every book would be a Penguin, a bird with a certain
'dignified flippancy', and a friendly invitation to anyone who
wished to spend their time reading.

In 1935, the first ten Penguin paperbacks were published.
Just a year later, three million Penguins had made their
way onto our shelves.

Reading was changed forever.

—

A lot has changed since 1935, including Penguin, but in the
most important ways we're still the same. We still believe that
books and reading are for everyone. And we still believe that
whether you're seeking an afternoon's escape, a vigorous debate
or a soothing bedtime story, all possibilities open with a book.

Whoever you are, whatever you're looking for,
you can find it with Penguin.